menue

the PALOMINO ✫ PONY ON PARADE

OLIVIA TUFFIN

nosy crow

With special thanks to Michelle Misra

First published 2015 by Nosy Crow Ltd
The Crow's Nest, 10a Lant Street
London SE1 1QR
www.nosycrow.com

ISBN: 978 0 85763 556 3

A CIP catalogue record for this book is available from the British Library.

Printed and bound in the UK by Clays Ltd, St Ives Plc.
Typeset by Tiger Media, Bishops Stortford, Hertfordshire

Papers used by Nosy Crow are made from wood grown in
sustainable forests.

1 3 5 7 9 8 6 4 2

For Lara, as always.
O.T.

PROLOGUE

The girl leaned forward in her seat, captivated by the scene below her. Here she was at the Horse of the Year Show, and she was watching the Mountain and Moorland Championship from the most expensive seats in the house! There was one pony she couldn't keep her eyes off – the most beautiful palomino mare – ridden by a girl who looked about her own age. The pony was breathtaking. Opening her catalogue, the girl carefully circled the palomino's stud name in the programme: "Carlamu Lily".

Watching the show proceed, she opened her eyes wider as a handsome groom appeared from the ringside to assist the little palomino and her jockey. Dressed in his funny flat cap and tweed waistcoat, he was unlike any boy she'd seen.

"Perfect," she whispered under her breath. She turned to her assistant and murmured something into her ear. The young woman nodded, tapping away on her phone.

Sitting back, the girl smiled contentedly. She had seen what she wanted, and she *always* got what she wanted…

CHAPTER ONE

"Calm down, Lily... Easy, girl..." Georgia murmured to her pony, patting the palomino's neck before unclipping the lead rein and letting her off across the field. Lily snorted, her breath hanging in a silver plume. Pawing at the ground, she sent up white flurries of powdery snow before launching herself into an extended trot. She was followed by her companions – Wilson, Callie and Santa. Their joy at being outside was clear to see.

The whole of the country was in the grip of a freezing-cold spell, so the ponies at Redgrove Farm were lucky to be getting some turnout. Georgia had heard of some who'd had to stay in their stables since the snow fell a couple of weeks ago. Georgia had helped Melanie and Simon, the owners of the yard, to dig out and salt a path to allow them to lead the ponies safely out towards the paddocks.

Heads aloft now, their tails streaming behind them, the ponies were in heaven, playing in the snow. Lily had been clipped for the Horse of the Year Show, and her golden coat was paler than usual. All the ponies were all wearing at least two rugs, apart from Callie the Exmoor pony, whose thick double coat gave her all the protection she needed.

"This winter season's almost tropical for

4

Callie," Melanie commented from Georgia's side. "Compared to life on the moor where she was born!"

"Isn't it?" grinned Georgia.

The two of them leaned on the gateway in companionable silence, observing the ponies as they cavorted and spun in the powder. It was lovely to watch them stretch their legs and use up some energy after being cooped up for so long. Even the normally laid-back Wilson had started to become a little restless in the stable, used to his daily turnout routine. Georgia rubbed her hands together now, blowing on them to try and warm her numb fingers. It was only early December but the news reports were all saying it could be the coldest winter on record, with lots more snow to come.

Georgia missed riding. Lily had had a couple of weeks off following her second place at the Horse of the Year Show, but Georgia would need to keep her fit. After all, Lily would be going to Olympia soon, having received a late qualification for the show!

"So is Dan coming over to the yard this afternoon?" asked Melanie.

"I'm actually going to meet him at the farm," said Georgia, her thoughts turning to her friend, who lived just down the road. She hoped his cows and sheep were OK. They'd been tucked up in the barn when Georgia had been round a couple of days ago, their breath steaming as they'd quietly munched on their hay. She smiled to herself, as she always did when she thought of Dan. They had been through so much together, with a bit of a rocky stage back in September when Georgia wouldn't admit how nervous she was before the Horse of the Year Show. Still, Dan, like the loyal friend he was, had stood by her. Even though

the PALOMINO ✿ PONY

Becky Hanbury, the prettiest but most annoying girl in their school year, had stepped up her flirting by several notches, he had still hung around with Georgia. Her best friend, Emma, was constantly asking if Dan was her boyfriend, to which Georgia normally answered with a blush and a shrug of her shoulders!

"Bet you wish we had an indoor school now, eh, Georgia," Melanie smiled, interrupting Georgia's thoughts as she pulled the scarf up around her nose.

"Oh, I don't mind too much," Georgia said truthfully. It would be amazing to be able to ride and school in the warm and dry but she was just enjoying riding when she could. She wasn't even nervous about the upcoming Olympia, just excited. And even without riding, there were plenty of yard jobs she could get on with – from sorting the endless pile of rugs in the tack room, to grooming the ponies. She didn't mind, she just loved being at Redgrove.

"So what have you and Dan got planned for later?" Melanie asked, satisfied that the ponies were now settled.

"Just hanging out," Georgia said as they walked back to the yard, picking their way carefully along the dug-out path. Georgia felt herself blush and was glad her scarf was pulled up around her face.

Melanie smiled. "That's nice," she said. "He's a good kid."

Just then, another boy sauntered into the yard, dressed in bright-blue salopettes and a bobble hat. It was Will Bowen, owner of star pony Santa, who was being stabled at the yard.

"You look like you're off to the ski slopes!" Georgia laughed.

"No, that's next weekend!" Will joked, flashing a quick grin at her.

the PALOMINO PONY

This could have come across as cocky, but Georgia knew it was all an act. Things had been tough for Will since he and his brother, the famous show rider Jasper Bowen, had moved back to the area following the loss of Jasper's sponsorship deal. Jasper was now teaching at the Round Barrow Pony Club, and he and his brother were in the process of converting the old stable block at the back of their cottage so they could eventually house Santa there. For the moment, the little mare was settled in the yard. She and Lily were the best of friends!

"No riding again today then?" Will said, cheerfully gesturing towards the ponies, who had settled down to eat the sweet piles of hay that Georgia and Melanie had left out for them.

Georgia shook her head. She really missed being able to take Lily out every day! As if reading her mind, Will pulled out a crumpled piece of paper and showed it to Georgia. "Here," he said. "Are you taking Lily to this?"

"What is it?" Georgia quickly scanned the paper in his hand, frowning slightly. "Christmas Eve Mock Hunt," she read aloud. "I don't know…" She looked at Melanie questioningly.

"Oh, Georgia, you should!" Melanie said, taking the paper and reading it. "Lily would really love it. Sophie could take Wilson as well – give the old boy a blast! She'll be back from university by then."

Georgia nodded slowly, thinking of Melanie's daughter, Sophie.

Will grinned, clearly pleased that Melanie liked the idea. "Jasper's organising it for the Pony Club," he said proudly. "What do you think, Georgia?"

Georgia thought for a few seconds. "I don't know," she said again in a small voice. "I don't know if hunting's really my thing." She loved animals and she felt a bit funny about chasing foxes around the countryside.

Will laughed, but not unkindly. "Don't worry, Georgia, we're not chasing anything. Well, we are, but nothing to do with animals anyway. That's why it's called a mock hunt. Jasper's got a cross-country runner from the Pony Club to carry the scent. It'll just be a good, fast cross-country ride over the countryside. The ponies will love it."

Thinking it over, imagining cantering Lily over the open fields, popping over jumps, her friends beside her, Georgia smiled. Actually, it sounded great! Plus it wasn't until Christmas Eve, which was still a few weeks away. Olympia would be over by then, so there'd be plenty of time for some fun! "Sure," she said finally. "Let's do it!"

"All right!" Will exclaimed, high-fiving her. Georgia couldn't help but grin at his excitement. Another event to look forward to over Christmas. She couldn't wait!

CHAPTER TWO

There was just enough time for Georgia to shower and change before going to meet Dan that afternoon. She and Will had mucked out all four boxes and moved what felt like hundreds of bales of hay to the feed store so that they could make up the evening feeds, and have a few bales in reserve in case the snow fell again. As she climbed into clean clothes, Georgia reflected on just how much had changed. She had *hated* Will when he had first come to Redgrove, and now they were good friends. It wasn't like it was with Dan though. Georgia's tummy lurched just a little bit as she locked the front door to the cottage, as it always did when she thought of seeing Dan. It wasn't like they were boyfriend and girlfriend … but he was special.

Georgia whistled for Pip, her spaniel, to join her. The afternoon stretched ahead without Lily and Wilson to ride, so she had arranged to hang out at the farm. The animals were all inside while the snow lay on the ground so Georgia knew there would be some work to do, but she also hoped that she and Dan might get to have a hot chocolate together in the farm shop. As she opened the garden gate, she looked down at her bare hands and realised her warm gloves were still on top of the counter by the sink. Telling Pip to sit, she rushed back in to grab them. As she picked them up, her eyes were drawn to an official-looking envelope, addressed to her, propped up against a jug. It must have come in the post when Georgia was over at the yard that morning.

Stuffing the envelope into her jacket pocket, she grabbed Pip's lead and set off towards Dan's farm, snow crunching underfoot. Pip ran ahead, barking with delight as she twirled and spun in the white powder. Georgia smiled at her dog, whose puppy-like enthusiasm for the snow was infectious.

Dan was checking a small flock of sheep when she arrived, filling their water buckets and putting fresh hay into their racks. They weren't far off lambing and were safely in the old stone barn to the side of the farm buildings, a little way from the house. Their fleeces were almost as white as the snow that had banked up around the walls outside. Dan was wearing a boiler suit underneath a wax jacket and had a wool hat pulled almost over his eyes. He grinned when he saw Georgia and gave her a little wave.

She let herself into the barn quietly, so as to not to disturb the ewes. Georgia had left Pip in the shelter of the porch with Dan's collie, Hattie. These sheep were Dan's very own – his dad had wanted to give him his own project so had handed over the responsibility to him. Georgia knew he took it very seriously and was really looking forward to the first lambs. Dan was fiercely protective of them, especially since there had been a couple of reports of sheep rustling in the local area in the build-up towards Christmas. Dan's dad had laughed off his concerns, reassuring him the criminals would be more interested in the big commercial flocks than a few pet ewes. The sheep, some as tame as Pip, pressed their warm noses against Georgia as she made her way over to Dan.

The stable next door was where Lily's foal, Secret, had been born during the Redgrove floods, so she always thought of him when she was in this part of the farm. Secret was now living down the road at Josephine Smalley's yard, ridden by Josephine's daughter, Alice, but Georgia still got to see him often.

"Hey, Georgia." Dan waved, his voice muffled under his scarf. "Give us a hand over here, will you?"

"Sure," Georgia said, smiling as she pulled off a section of hay and set to work. She thought of Emma, who was probably curled up indoors with her laptop, watching a film. She and Emma might be best friends but they had very different interests. Georgia enjoyed the odd day's shopping in town with Emma, but much preferred hanging out at Redgrove or on Dan's farm. Luckily, when it was sunny Emma often came to Redgrove to ride, although Georgia suspected it might have more to do with Will being there than to ride the ponies!

"Not far off now, are you, old girl." Dan was crouching next to one of the older ewes, a solid, pretty sheep with a speckled face and kind eyes. Georgia knew she was special – Dan had hand-reared her. Georgia had enjoyed hearing the tales of the lamb's antics as a youngster, as tame as Hattie. Dan had even sneaked the lamb into his bedroom once or twice, and the two of them had watched cartoons together. Now older, she was expecting her last set of twins, and Dan was making sure he took extra-special care of her. She was then going to be allowed a good retirement.

When the sheep had been fed and their water topped up, Dan turned to Georgia. "Shall we go down to the farm shop? Get a hot drink?"

"Sure," said Georgia.

The two friends made their way out of the barn

and walked up the drive. The surrounding roads had been cleared by the snow ploughs but even so, the only vehicles in the car park were 4x4s, able to easily tackle the icy conditions.

Settling into a quiet corner, Dan made Georgia her favourite hot chocolate. Dan was full of enthusiasm, clearly bursting to tell Georgia something.

"So have you seen what's going on in the top meadows?" he said finally, his eyes shining. It was obviously something exciting! Georgia hadn't heard there was anything going on in the rolling parkland beyond Seven Birches – the yard where her friend Lexie had lived briefly. She shook her head, puzzled, as Dan rolled his eyes.

"Honestly, Georgia, I thought you'd be the first to know. I'm amazed Emma didn't tell you!" He paused for dramatic effect. "They're filming a real-life movie down there!"

"Really?" Georgia frowned. "I can't believe I haven't heard about it!" This was exciting news for their sleepy village.

"Yup," Dan continued. "Georgia, there's horses, loads of them!" He grinned. "Me and Ben walked over to watch. It's some sort of fairytale film, maybe a kids' movie."

Georgia's ears pricked up. Anything that involved horses was always bound to catch her attention. "Cool!" she enthused. "Wonder what the horses are like."

"Trust you to ask that." Dan grinned, nudging her.

The two of them chatted for a while longer, agreeing that they would go down at some point and watch the filming. Georgia told Dan about the Pony Club Christmas Eve Mock Hunt and Lily's play in the snow that morning, while Dan chatted about his little flock of sheep.

"So cool, Georgia. I can't wait for the lambs," Dan laughed.

Georgia was glad that he hadn't mentioned Becky Hanbury in the whole of their conversation, aware that her classmate had been texting Dan most days and inviting him to all the Christmas parties. Last week she had even asked if he wanted to go to the cinema, right in front of Georgia, who had just stood there as Becky had completely ignored her. She couldn't say anything, not really. It wasn't like Dan was actually her boyfriend! Luckily Dan had politely declined all the invitations, but even so, girls like Becky didn't give up easily, and Dan was becoming a lot more popular all of a sudden.

Remembering the mysterious letter that had been propped up on the kitchen sideboard, she pulled it out of her pocket and laid it on the table in front of them. Dan reached over to look.

"What's that?" he said curiously.

Georgia shrugged, turning the thick cream envelope over in her hands. "I don't know," she said. "It was there when I got back from the yard."

"Well, go on then." Dan craned his neck forward, looking at the official stamp on the envelope. "Open it!"

Slowly, Georgia slid her finger under the envelope's flap and pulled out a letter. Frowning, she read the first couple of lines and then glanced up at Dan, a puzzled expression on her face. "It's about Lily."

Instantly, Dan looked worried. "Oh no," he said nervously. "Nothing bad? Not Jemma again?" he said, referring to Lily's previous owner.

Georgia frowned and looked back down at the letter, reading more.

"Dear Miss G. Black and Carlamu Lily." Reading aloud, Georgia traced the writing with her index finger as she tried to make sense of the words. *"We*

21

are a production company currently making a film in the south of England with some scenes in the village of Redgrove, specifically chosen for its beautiful location and rich equestrian heritage. The film involves horses, which are mostly sourced from a specialist company that trains equines in the world of film. However, one particular scene calls for the young actress to ride in on a palomino horse. Our client has specifically requested Carlamu Lily, after closely following her progress at the Horse of the Year Show. Of course we would be willing to offer a fee…"

Georgia stopped there, speechless. She looked up from the letter to Dan and back again. Turning her hands over, she realised they were actually shaking.

"Oh my goodness!" Dan was practically jumping up and down on his seat with excitement. "Lily's going to be a film star!"

CHAPTER THREE

Quickly, Georgia read the rest of the letter. Filming of this scene was due to commence shortly and if the real snow had melted, then fake snow would be used. An exact location was still to be found. Lily was only going to need to walk with the actress, and no stunt work was required.

"So what sort of fee are they talking about?" Dan asked.

Georgia's eyes flicked down and she read on. Her hands started to tremble. "Two thousand pounds…"

"Two thousand pounds!" Dan cried out.

"Yes," said Georgia in a shaky voice. Two thousand pounds! It was such a lot of money. Lily needed all sorts of new things and it would help her mother with the mortgage payment on their little cottage. Georgia's heart leapt, and then fell again.

"What is it?" Dan asked, seeing the look on her face.

"I dunno," said Georgia. "It's just…" She hesitated.

She knew this was a once-in-a-lifetime opportunity for Lily, but something didn't feel quite right. "It's just… Well, I'm the only person who's ever ridden Lily since she was bought from the Carlamu stud," she said slowly.

"Yes," said Dan. "But they're only talking about walking with her, and no stunt work."

"Well, Lily's not officially mine," Georgia said. "She's only mine on loan. Melanie's her real owner. I'd need to get permission from her. And I just feel a bit funny about anyone else riding Lily…"

It was clear that Dan could not see her point at all. "Don't be silly!" he exclaimed, still bursting with excitement. "Lily will be fine, and you'll get paid! Think of the things you can buy for Lily. Plus, she'll be in an actual film!"

Georgia nodded silently, before agreeing that she would ask Melanie.

"Well, come on then!" Dan said. "Let's go to the yard now! You need to get the horses in, right?"

Georgia nodded again, feeling a little dazed; she still couldn't quite take in what she had read. Jumping up, Dan grabbed her hand and they ran out into the freezing air. The sky was starting to look dusky, even though it was only mid-afternoon. Dan was right, the ponies did need to come back in for the evening, as more snow was forecast.

Georgia and Dan ran down the lane from the farm and along the main road. Turning the corner to Redgrove, they headed up the driveway. As they trudged over the top meadow, Pip and Hattie running and sniffing ahead, Georgia still couldn't quite believe it. Lily – *her* Lily – had been selected to star in a film!

✩ ✩ ✩

Passing Wilson's and Callie's head collars to Dan, Georgia and Dan set off for the paddock to get the ponies in. All four were waiting by the gate. Callie was furiously pawing at the snow, impatient to get back to her warm stable and big hay net. Lily, next to Santa, whickered softly when she saw Georgia. She did the same every day, and Georgia's heart melted each and every time. The little palomino was so beautiful that she didn't quite seem real. No wonder she had been star-spotted by the film company!

Soon the ponies were settled in their stables and Georgia saw Melanie striding across the yard, wrapped up in a black wool cape. Sophie, her daughter, trotted behind her, wearing furry earmuffs over her pink-streaked hair and looking as stylish as ever! She had broken up for the Christmas holidays from university.

"Melanie!" Dan waved her over. "Georgia's got something exciting to tell you!"

"Oh, really?" Melanie looked intrigued. Georgia handed over the letter. It took just a few moments for Melanie to scan through it, and then she handed it back to Georgia with a smile.

"Well," she said. "It certainly is exciting. How do you feel about it though?"

Georgia smiled. Melanie knew her so well.

She could see how she wasn't sharing Dan's enthusiasm. Sophie, on the other hand, had read the letter too and was squealing with excitement!

"I don't know," Georgia said quietly, tracing an "O" in the snow with her yard boots. "I just feel a bit funny about the thought of someone else riding her, that's all."

Melanie nodded. Taking Georgia's arm, she led her a little way away from the others so they could talk on their own.

"You've worked so hard at regaining Lily's trust," said Melanie. "But Lily is tougher than she looks. She behaved impeccably at the Horse of the Year Show – even with the overwhelming atmosphere – and she's generally happy for me, Dan, Sophie or Will to handle her. You know, I think Lily will be fine – as long as you're there."

"I guess," said Georgia. "So you'd be happy for her to do it?"

"I would," said Melanie. "And by the way – in case you're wondering – the two-thousand-pound fee would be yours. I might be her official owner, but you are in every other way. Just think about it, Georgia," she said kindly. "I'm happy as long as you are."

Georgia nodded.

"Would it make you feel better," Sophie chipped in, "if you met the actress first, before you decide? Then you can see if you think she would be right for Lily."

"That's a good idea," Georgia agreed. She knew she was being precious about the palomino mare, but Sophie's idea made sense. The girl could be a horse lover, just like her. She couldn't write off the offer just yet. Especially as the money would come in very useful!

CHAPTER FOUR

Once Georgia had agreed to meet the actress who would ride Lily, things progressed quickly. Melanie took charge and emailed back and forth with the production company. The actress, whose identity was top secret, was going to come to the yard the following weekend to see Lily and meet everyone at the stables.

And there was good news on the weather

the PALOMINO ✧PONY

front – the snow had stopped for a while and was gradually starting to melt, which meant that Georgia was able to ride out again. That morning, instead of turning Lily out, Georgia spent ages brushing her golden coat and combing out her creamy mane and tail.

Lily had been carefully clipped by Melanie a few weeks ago and her pale coat felt like brushed velvet. Will joined Georgia to finish tacking up his dark-brown mare Santa in the yard, a cheerful jade and white silk on his skullcap brightening up the winter day. Georgia smoothed Lily's dark-blue wool exercise sheet over her muscled hindquarters and, fastening her chinstrap, led the little mare out into the cobbled yard and swung lightly into the saddle. They were only going to ride around the quiet lanes of Redgrove, as there was still snow lying in the frozen fields and on the downs, but it felt amazing to be back in the saddle. Lily obviously agreed – her ears were pricked as she walked out in perfect stride with Santa, both jigging slightly sideways with eagerness, the cold air making them both a little fresh.

Will and Georgia chatted easily as they hacked through the centre of the village, passing the old thatched pub and the driveway up to Dan's farm. The high street looked really pretty in the early December sunshine and several people stopped to admire the ponies. When Lily had been at the Horse of the Year Show, the local paper had run a story on the palomino's rescue and journey to the Championships, so she was a bit of a celebrity now. Jasper had organised for the Round Barrow Pony Club members to come along to watch Lily's performance at Olympia. So it felt as though all eyes were on the little palomino pony!

"She'll be even more famous when she's a film

star!" Will chuckled, reins in one hand like a cowboy, Santa's head low and relaxed. Like Dan, he had found the news really exciting.

"Hmmm," Georgia said, reaching forward to pat Lily. She was still unconvinced.

Emma was waiting in the yard when the two ponies clattered up the drive. Wrapped in a quilted scarlet coat, a white bobble hat over her shiny dark-brown hair, she blushed a bit when she saw Will, who grinned back at her as he untacked Santa. It was so obvious Emma liked him – she even helped him muck out sometimes, and Emma *only* mucked out when she really had to! She was also brimming with excitement about the filming and had been down that morning watching the proceedings with her mum.

"You've *got* to let Lily be in the film," she bubbled enthusiastically. "Do you know the name of the actress yet?"

Georgia shook her head. Everyone wanted Lily to be the star of the show. Everyone except her! Lily rubbed Georgia's arm with her golden head before resting her nose on Georgia's shoulder, leaving a trail of white foam and blowing out through her nostrils. Georgia hated to admit it, but she really wanted to keep the little pony all to herself. What if Lily became *really* famous? Then Melanie might want to sell her.

Georgia sighed. She knew she was being irrational, but the little pony meant the absolute world to her and there was always a fear at the back of her mind that one day she would be taken away. With a second place at the Horse of the Year Show and a qualification for Olympia, Georgia didn't like to think how much the little pony must be worth. Thousands and thousands of pounds, probably. Pushing the thought to the back of her mind, she sighed. She had never imagined when she stumbled across Lily on a school trip that things would work out like this!

☆ ☆ ☆

Georgia had thought about what the actress would be like, but as it turned out Jocelyn McCall-Jones was nothing like she had imagined. It was early on Saturday morning when the actress arrived at Redgrove. Over the last few days, Georgia had built up the meeting in her head and was half expecting a white limo to purr up the drive and a fur-coated glamorous blonde to sweep out, wearing dark sunglasses. So she was slightly taken aback to walk into the large farmhouse kitchen of Melanie's house and be greeted by a small fair-haired girl, dressed quite normally in jeans and a white shirt.

Jocelyn was undeniably pretty – Sophie was gaping at her from her position perched on top of the Aga, hands curled around a cup of tea. Georgia wasn't really that up to date with who was who in the celebrity world so she didn't recognise her. Georgia guessed she was a couple of years older than her – maybe sixteen or seventeen.

Jocelyn leapt to her feet as Georgia arrived, and the two girls shook hands. It felt very strange to have the actress right here in Melanie's kitchen, among the terriers, and the rosettes, and the saddle soap on the table! Jocelyn had two assistants with her, who were hovering around the kitchen; one seemed to be flicking through emails on an expensive-looking phone.

"I'm Joss," Jocelyn said finally in a cut-glass accent, so refined and polished it rang around the huge farmhouse kitchen like a bell.

"And I'm Georgia." Georgia smiled back, silently thankful that Joss wasn't as tall as she had imagined. Lily only stood at just over thirteen hands and was very slightly built, so it was better if someone light would be riding her.

"You're so lucky to have such a lovely pony!"
Joss gushed. "Lily's so beautiful!" she continued
dreamily, her eyes sparkling. "You know, I was
watching you at the Horse of the Year Show?"

Georgia shook her head, the situation feeling
more and more surreal.

"I was in one of the private boxes," Joss explained.
"And as soon as I saw Lily I *knew* she was the
pony for me. Well, for the film anyway," she
added. "I mean, I knew that I didn't want any
other pony, so my assistant sorted it all out." She
grinned.

"Well, er, that's great," Georgia said, prickling
already.

"Well now," Melanie said, pulling on a coat.
"Why don't we go and meet the little star?"

"Great!" Joss smiled. She whirled around the
kitchen, reminding Georgia of a pixie, or a fairy – she
didn't just walk, she sort of danced and pirouetted

everywhere. Georgia felt positively clumsy as she pulled on her ancient wellies and followed Joss and Melanie out into the garden where snow still lay in the shade. Despite the recent thaw it was still freezing and the cold air made Georgia's eyes sting. Lily was waiting in her stable next to Santa, and both ponies hung their heads over their doors gazing in interest as Melanie opened the gates on to the yard from the garden.

Lily gave a whicker when she caught sight of Georgia, and Joss gasped in appreciation as they neared the palomino. Georgia knew she looked good from a distance, just as she must have done from Joss's box at the Horse of the Year Show. But close up, Lily was exquisite, like a china figurine. It was little wonder that at eleven years old she was one of the country's top Welsh Section Bs.

"Have you heard of her?" Georgia whispered to Sophie as soon as Joss was out of earshot.

"Of course I've heard of her!" Sophie raised her eyebrows. "She was in that film *Just Waiting for You*, and lots of other TV stuff, though I can't think what off the top of my head. But she's definitely an up-and-coming actress."

"Oh," said Georgia quietly. She could see why. Joss certainly had presence!

"So, Joss," Melanie said as the actress reached up to pat Lily on her neck. "How much horsey experience do you have?"

"Well, I love horses more than anything," Joss said vaguely, with a huge smile.

"OK," Melanie said slowly. "But I mean, do you have lessons? Have you got a horse?" she questioned further. Georgia knew that Melanie wouldn't mind if Joss was a novice, but she needed to know so that they could correctly prepare Lily.

Joss nodded. "I've had lessons," she said

confidently. "My instructor says I could be really good."

Georgia didn't doubt Joss loved horses – it was clear the way she gazed at Lily and softly stroked her muzzle, but could she actually ride a horse? There was only one way to find out. Reaching for Lily's head collar, Georgia slipped it on over her nose and led the little pony out on to the yard. Handing Joss a bridle, she quickly put the saddle on, did up the girth and gave Lily a quick pat before turning back to Joss, who was still holding the bridle, now upside down, looking hesitant.

Feeling a bit awkward, Georgia took the bridle from her and quickly slipped it over the little mare's head. Perhaps Joss just hadn't been taught to tack up when she had lessons, which was understandable.

Melanie was going to assess Joss and Lily together in the small outdoor arena. Georgia led

Lily out of the yard and through the gates into the sand school. Joss was wearing expensive-looking jeans and long patent-leather riding boots over the top of them. Georgia didn't like to think how much they cost. Hundreds of pounds, she imagined, looking down at her wellingtons.

Still, she had to admit, Joss was nice, much nicer than she'd imagined her to be. And she didn't seem to be snobby or stuck up at all, although she did seem to rely on her assistants for everything. One was now holding on to her bobble hat like it was a precious diamond, as Joss adjusted her skullcap.

Using the mounting block, Joss reached a leg over the saddle and was soon sitting on Lily. She picked up the reins and sat up straight. Her position was pretty good, but very stiff. Still, Georgia was relieved to see that she didn't haul Lily in the mouth or kick her to move forward. She just sat there.

A bit hesitant, Lily looked almost bemused at the lack of direction from her rider. Thinking fast, Georgia stepped forward and clucked lightly under her tongue, and Lily, used to groundwork with Georgia, walked politely forward. Now that she had met Joss, and thought about the chance for Lily to star in the film, Georgia thought that she would quite like it to happen, even though it was obvious that Joss was a complete beginner. Joss squealed with delight as Lily completed a twenty-metre circle, with Georgia walking ahead, encouraging the little mare forward.

Halting next to Melanie, Joss reached forward and hugged Lily tightly around her neck. "She's definitely the perfect pony!" she enthused. "Thank you so much!"

Georgia grinned. If all Lily had to do was walk on set and if all Joss had to do was sit there, Georgia could cope with that! "No problem," she said, and she meant it. Running her hands lightly over Lily's small ears, she felt a thrill of excitement. Her pony, who Georgia had rescued, was going to be a film star. She couldn't quite believe it!

CHAPTER FIVE

Joss didn't seem in any particular hurry to leave
Redgrove Farm, even when Lily had been untacked
and Georgia had put her back in her stable. Joss's
assistants were still in the kitchen, talking into
their mobile phones and emailing furiously at the
big farmhouse table. First, Joss wanted to meet
Wilson and Callie and Santa, and then she wanted
to watch Georgia fill the afternoon's hay nets. She

seemed fascinated by everything, asking loads of questions. Will then joined them in the yard, ready to school Santa while the weather was better. Joss's eyes lit up when she saw him, and soon Will was cantering Santa in a relaxed circle in the school, reins in one hand as always.

"Oh," said Joss suddenly. "He's nice!"

Then Georgia heard the sound of the gate being pulled back and Dan walked into the yard, for once not in his boiler suit but wearing an old tweed jacket and jeans. Immediately Joss's attention was drawn to him. Flashing a megawatt smile, Joss stuck out her hand to greet him with a handshake and Georgia noted the perfectly manicured nails and sparkly watch. Looking down at her own bitten nails and hands rough from so many years of gripping reins and mucking out, she quickly stuck them in her pockets.

"I'm Joss," the actress purred at Dan, who looked

45

bemused. A slight smile lifted at the corner of Georgia's mouth as she realised Dan had no idea who Joss was.

"Dan, this is Jocelyn – Joss – McCall-Jones. She's come to try Lily out for the film," said Georgia.

"Ah," Dan said politely. "So you're the actress? Well, hi, Joss. So what did you think of our little pony?"

"She's *perfect*," Joss trilled. "I'm so pleased Georgia is letting me have her! She's the only pony I wanted."

Georgia frowned slightly at this. Lily was only going to be Joss's for one day; she certainly wasn't *having* her!

Dan must have picked up on this because he winked at Georgia and immediately she felt embarrassed, knowing she was just being silly.

"Soooo, tell me all about it!" Emma was beside herself with excitement when she joined Dan and Georgia at the yard later that afternoon, as they finished the mucking out. Reluctantly, Joss had finally left with her assistants, as she had some scenes to film that afternoon. Georgia couldn't decide if it was Lily or Dan that had caused her to hang around the yard for hours. She had asked loads of questions about keeping a horse, some really silly ones! Remembering that she had also been a novice not so long ago, Georgia had done her best to answer her without sounding patronising.

"So what's she like in real life?" Em asked now. "Did she like Lily? Could she ride?" Emma was completely overexcited, firing questions at Georgia.

"Nice, yes and no, not really," she answered as truthfully as possible. While Dan was out of earshot she thought about telling Emma how Joss had immediately latched on to Dan, but decided not to, knowing it made her sound jealous. Dan was handsome and always nice to people when he met them, so girls normally liked him. She sighed. She was probably worrying unnecessarily.

☆ ☆ ☆

If Georgia had been in any doubt about Joss's crush on Dan, it was soon made very clear indeed! A few days later, when Joss returned to Redgrove with the film's producer to discuss Lily's scenes, Dan was the first person she asked to see. She had already been back earlier that week to check out the bottom meadow to see if it was suitable for filming Lily's scene. Dan had been there then as well, and Joss had ended up alone with him in the barn as he filled the hay nets. Georgia had been going back and forth bringing the ponies in. Typically it was the night she was wearing an old boiler suit of Dan's, with straw tangled in her hair. In contrast, Joss had looked so polished in her tight white jeans and black parka with fur trim, her hair piled loosely on top of her head. There had been a lot of laughter between Dan and Joss that night. Now, standing in the yard, Georgia noticed Joss's eyes darting around, looking for Dan. "Where's your friend?" she asked in a casual way.

Georgia felt her hackles rise. By referring to Dan casually as her friend, Georgia felt as though she was dismissing what she and Dan had between them. Joss wasn't to know, of course, that Dan and Georgia had a special friendship, but it made Georgia feel uneasy all the same. "He's probably looking after the sheep, or helping his dad," she said quietly.

"Oh, right." Joss tilted her head slightly. "You are so lucky," she beamed. "Having such a good *friend*. Dan said you were like a little sister to him."

Joss's words sounded innocent enough, but Georgia couldn't help but feel taken aback. A *sister*? She thought there was a bit more to their friendship than that.

Trying not to show her hurt, she smiled weakly. "Did he?" she replied, busying herself with hanging up the lead ropes. If that's how Dan felt, then she couldn't change that.

"Oh yes," Joss continued sweetly, seemingly unaware of the effect her words were having on Georgia. "He said it was *so* nice being good friends with a non-girly girl who loved getting mucky and doing all the dirty jobs!"

Was that really how Dan saw her? Replaying Joss's words over and over in her mind later that evening, Georgia studied her reflection in the hall mirror, next to the framed photo of her riding

Lily at the Horse of the Year Show. As usual, her dark-blonde hair was tangled and windswept, and, looking carefully, Georgia noticed a streak of creosote across her forehead, from where she had been helping Melanie mend the paddock fencing earlier. Walking past and carrying an armful of clean washing, Mrs Black paused at the sight of her daughter's serious expression.

"All OK, sweetheart?" she asked, and Georgia nodded.

"Mum?" she asked quizzically, and then paused, not sure how to phrase the question. "Do you think I'm a non-girly girl?"

Mrs Black burst out laughing, kissing her daughter on her freckled forehead. "Well, you're certainly not afraid to get your hands dirty, if that's what you mean. But that's part of your charm," she smiled. "And anyway," she said, gesturing towards the photo of the little palomino, "Lily wouldn't want you any other way."

So her mum clearly thought it too. Georgia turned back to her reflection, drawing herself up tall. Still, Lily didn't care what she looked like or how she acted. If all Dan saw her as was a little sister, then she would just have to live with that.

CHAPTER SIX

"All OK?" Dan and Georgia had been working beside each other in silence for most of the next evening as they sorted the Redgrove ponies for the night, fluffing up the beds and topping up water buckets. Dan often came over to help and normally Georgia enjoyed his company. This time, Joss's words were still ringing in her ears, and she couldn't help but feel a little grumpy. She busied herself doing up the leg straps on Lily's rug as he leaned on her stable door.

"Fine," she muttered, not looking at him.

"You know, there's a Pony Club party after the Mock Hunt," Dan continued casually. "Will you be going?"

Georgia *had* heard that there was a party and normally would have suggested that she and Dan go to the party together, but instead she decided to keep her cool. "I expect so," she said airily. "I might ask Will if he wants to go with me and Em."

For a split second, Georgia saw a look of total confusion cross Dan's face. Quickly, Georgia reached under Lily's tummy to adjust her straps.

"OK," he said, drumming his fingers on the stable door. "That sounds like fun."

If Georgia had glanced up, she would have noticed the hurt in Dan's eyes, but instead she concentrated hard on Lily's rug, refusing to look at her friend.

☆ ☆ ☆

On the morning Lily was due to shoot her scene, Georgia felt as nervous as if she was competing in a big horse show. It was still pitch black outside and, drawing back her striped curtains, she stared out into the darkness, squinting as she watched the snowflakes curl and drift down on to the frozen lawn below the window.

Georgia was grateful the filming was going to take place at Melanie's yard so that they didn't have to risk boxing Lily anywhere in this weather. And the producers had been in raptures over the bottom meadow at the yard, which bordered the small wood. It would look especially good in the snow, they had said.

The bottom meadow was Georgia's favourite place on the farm; it was where she had ridden

Lily for the first time, and where she had gone when the pressure building up to the Horse of the Year Show was getting too much. It was a place that she liked to be if she just needed time to think.

Since Joss's meetings at Redgrove Farm, the emails to Melanie had been flying backward and forward from the film company. They wanted Lily in a simple snaffle and no saddle, which was fine – Lily was used to being schooled and ridden bareback. A bit trickier was the fact that Joss would be riding in a billowing hooded cape – something Georgia had been trying to work on in the few days she'd had to practise with Lily. She had improvised with an old picnic rug fastened around her neck, and crossed her fingers that Lily would be sensible enough to accept it. The first time she had tried, Lily had snorted and bolted forward a few steps in the school, much to the amusement of Emma, who was watching on the sides. But gradually she had accepted the long fabric and happily walked, trotted and cantered in the school with the makeshift cape trailing behind her.

Quickly brushing her teeth and hair, Georgia dressed in her warmest clothes, pulling a fleecy headband over her ears. Her small room was full of mementos of Lily's adventures, including photographs and rosettes from the Horse of the Year Show, which had centre place on her crowded bookshelf. She paused, just for a second, as she always did, gazing at the photo of Lily cantering in the arena at the Championships.

Then, calling for Pip, she grabbed an apple from the fruit bowl before making her way outside. The air was strangely muffled as the snowflakes started to fall a little bit faster. At least the film company would get their snow now, and wouldn't have to spray fake snow all over Melanie's beautiful fields.

Dan was waiting for her on the corner at the end of her lane, snowflakes melting in his sandy hair. He grinned when he saw Georgia.

"All set?" he asked cheerfully, and Georgia nodded. It was quite romantic actually, walking to the yard in the snow with Dan beside her. Then she shook herself, remembering Dan had called her a "little sister". Any possible romance between them was obviously just in Georgia's head. As a result, she shrugged Dan's arm away when he put it around her shoulders and he flashed her a confused look.

There was no time to say anything though, as they had soon reached Redgrove. The yard was already alive with activity and light, despite the early start. There were trailers everywhere, flashier than the most luxurious horseboxes, and people milling around in long quilted jackets, clutching paper cups of coffee or shouting into little walkie-talkies.

"Wow…" Georgia let out a low whistle. The film company must have set up overnight, because Redgrove had looked quite normal when she had left the yard the previous evening. The ponies, all still in their stables, were watching the proceedings with interest. Luckily, all four of them were used to big shows in indoor arenas, so they were completely unfazed by the lights and noise. Callie, once a top show pony, looked the least concerned. She was never worried, as long as she had food!

"All right, my beauty?" Georgia called over to the little Exmoor.

The pony stuck her head out over the door as Georgia opened the yard gates, her fluffy forelock full of hay, before grabbing another mouthful, her eyes bright and shiny. Georgia chuckled, patting

Callie on her soft muzzle. Moving down the line of stables, greeting Wilson and Santa, Georgia reached Lily's box. The little mare was gazing at the bustle of activity with soft amber eyes. Her beautiful cream mane and tail were full of shavings, which clung to her wool rug like snowflakes.

Georgia had spent ages the day before washing her mane and tail with warm water, so all she needed to do was comb the shavings out with a soft body brush. Tying Lily up, she set to work and was soon engrossed in her grooming routine. Dan leaned over the stable door.

"Exciting, isn't it?" he grinned, brushing snowflakes off his damp hair.

But before Georgia could reply, she was interrupted by a squeal.

"Dan!"

It was Joss, and she was right beside him, tucking herself under his arm, and gazing up at him adoringly. She was looking especially glamorous today, her hair set in elaborate curls. Georgia felt so scruffy in comparison. Glancing down at her jeans and quilted jacket – complete with slobber stain from Lily – she wished she had spent more time on her appearance.

Dan smiled warmly. "Hey, Joss," he said cheerfully. Georgia couldn't help but notice that he was smiling at the actress with a big wide smile that was normally reserved for her.

"Brrrrr," Joss said in a tinkly voice, snuggling in closer. "Isn't it cold! I hope you're going to be around to watch me ride Lily later." She looked up at Dan under her long eyelashes, and Georgia felt her stomach churn. Joss was really nice, pretty and practically famous, so how could Dan *not* fall for her. After acting like her best friend when she first met her, it was as if Georgia didn't exist now. She glanced at Dan, hoping for one of his reassuring smiles but he was too busy laughing at something Joss said.

Turning back to Lily, who snuffled into her hand, Georgia felt a hard lump of jealousy rise in her throat. Then, giving herself a mental shake, she reminded herself that she was better than that. Besides, it was only short term – once the scenes were filmed then it would just be her and Dan, and Lily, and Olympia, and Christmas to look forward to. But a niggling seed of doubt had set in now. Joss's words kept running past her eyes, *a friend, like a sister*, and try as she might, Georgia just couldn't forget them.

CHAPTER SEVEN

"OK, everyone!" The producer, a tall dark-haired man in a baseball cap, called out, getting everyone to stop and tune in to what he was saying. His name was Brodie, and he was from America. Georgia had liked him straightaway when he'd first visited Redgrove. He had known exactly what colour Lily was, rather than just describing her as gold or biscuit-coloured, and after patting Lily for ages had confessed that he really missed ponies, having grown up on a ranch in Montana. That was why he had decided to make a film that had so many horses in it!

Now Georgia pulled back Lily's wool rug. Brodie let out a low whistle. "She's looking beautiful," he said admiringly, making Georgia think of Eric, Lily's breeder, and how proud he would be if he could see his pony now. It was a world away from the wet mountainside where Georgia had first met Lily. Who'd have thought the little mare would go on to compete at the Horse of the Year Show, go to Olympia and star in a film? It seemed as though there was nothing Lily couldn't do!

Melanie, Simon and Sophie were already waiting down in the bottom meadow. There were swarms of people rushing about, and a few 4×4 vehicles parked around. The snow was still drifting down. In the eerie half-light of the morning the bottom meadow and woods looked fantastic, just right for the scene. Joss was playing the part of a fairy, and Lily was cast as a mystical pony. A woman with bright-red hair, who had introduced herself as the wardrobe lady, had given Georgia some fine silver glitter to rub into Lily's mane and tail, which now glinted and sparkled against the snow. She did look magical, Georgia thought, crossing her fingers and hoping the glitter would wash out before Olympia. Giggling to herself, she imagined what Janey, the ultra-traditional instructor at the Round Barrow Pony Club, would say if she saw Lily now.

Lily, walking quietly beside her, wrapped up in two rugs until the last moment, surveyed the scene quietly. There was no sign of Joss – or Dan for that matter, Georgia thought, looking around. He had disappeared. She placed a hand on the palomino's neck, watching the snowflakes as they settled on her creamy mane. "Hope this is OK for you, girl," she whispered. Even though she knew Joss was only walking on Lily, she still felt strange about someone else riding her. Melanie had assured her that it was only because she had done such a good job gaining Lily's trust that someone else was now able to ride her, but even so.

Lily shifted her weight to her other foot as Georgia wriggled her toes in her yard boots, wondering if they would ever feel warm again. All of a sudden Joss descended on her like a whirlwind, followed by Dan, grinning from ear to ear. Georgia couldn't help but notice that he had completely changed outfits. He was even wearing a flat cap perched on his sandy hair.

"Georgia, you'll never guess what," he said breathlessly, and without waiting for her answer, he whooped, "I'm in the film!"

"W–what?" Georgia asked, confused, as Joss giggled.

"Well, Brodie thought Dan looked perfect for the part of a stable hand," Joss said. "So he's decided to add him in! It's all a bit last-minute. All he has to do is walk out with Lily, and then stop, while I ride on." She placed a hand on Dan's arm. "You'll be perfect, I know!" Then, looking straight at Georgia with a little smile, she added, "*I* had a small say in the casting, as well."

Once again, Georgia felt the knot of jealousy, all too familiar now, form in her stomach, only this time it almost winded her. She should be really happy for Dan – it was a brilliant thing for him to do. But she wished Joss didn't have to flirt with him so much, especially right in front of her!

"That's so cool, Dan," she said, forcing a smile on her face, but Dan was already engrossed in a conversation with Joss and Brodie now, all in a little huddle together.

Standing alone, Georgia suddenly wondered if

it was too late to back out, but she knew, realistically, that it was too far down the line for that. Besides, this was a chance for Lily to shine. She gritted her teeth. They were ready to start filming, and Joss removed the long quilted jacket she had been wearing, revealing a silver cape studded with sparkling stones. She looked sensational, and Georgia had to admit it would look really striking against Lily's cream coat. Glancing at Dan, she noticed him staring at Joss and her heart sank. He really liked her, it was obvious. And Joss really liked Dan. Georgia just couldn't compete with her. Feeling tears prick the corners of her eyes, Georgia hated herself for caring so much.

Calling Lily and Georgia forward, the director patted the little mare, who had been waiting so patiently as the snowflakes settled on her pale eyelashes, and explained what he wanted. One of the assistants carefully legged Joss up into the saddle. Georgia was relieved to see Lily stand stock-still while Joss rearranged her cape. All of Georgia's hard work with the picnic rug had clearly paid off. Then all of a sudden Georgia was surrounded by people and swept to the side as Dan, Lily and Joss took centre-stage. The little mare glanced back at Georgia, as if to seek approval, and Georgia felt a lump rise in her throat. She clucked quietly under her breath, hoping Lily sensed her.

"Right, everyone – action!" Brodie called, his Midwestern American twang cutting across the cold air.

Dan took hold of Lily's bridle, which was bedecked with crystals, and started to lead her forward. The little palomino walked obediently after him with Joss sitting bolt upright, a solemn expression on her pretty face. Reaching the edge of the wood, she halted Lily and to Georgia's utter shock leaned forward and kissed Dan lightly on the cheek. He stood back, gave a little bow and watched the pair as they rode on, Lily's hoof prints almost immediately covered by powder. Georgia was frozen to the spot. She felt winded all over again.

Brodie gave a sideways glance at her and chuckled. "Now, Georgia, come on," he said good-naturedly. "It's only acting. I thought it would add to the scene, that's all."

Georgia nodded miserably. What else could she do? Lily was on her way back now, but Brodie didn't seem satisfied. "The light," he said, peering through the cameraman's lens. "Let's shoot that a second time." Georgia's heart sank even further. She was going to have to watch the whole thing all over again!

☆ ☆ ☆

In the end, the scene had to be shot a further six times until Brodie was happy with the result. And each time Georgia felt her stomach turn as Joss turned to kiss Dan another six times. She couldn't help but notice that Dan was avoiding her eye as she stood miserably by the fence. The only good bit about the whole thing was that Lily was behaving beautifully. Georgia had to admit that she and Joss did look fantastic. Now that she knew that Lily was OK with everything, she began to wish that the little mare might just spook a bit and unseat Joss. She wouldn't look so perfect lying in the snow! No one else seemed to realise Georgia was upset; everyone was far too excited, even Sophie and Melanie, who normally noticed when Georgia was down. Will had joined her now, his sleek dark curls damp with snowflakes.

"Wow," he grinned, as Georgia started to lead Lily back to the stables. "Lucky Dan!" He wasn't trying to upset Georgia, but even so she couldn't help but glare at him a little bit.

Picking up on her mood, Will quickly changed the subject. "Lily's looking great, Georgia," he said cheerfully. "A real film star!"

"Isn't she?" Nodding, Georgia took hold of Lily's bridle. She could barely bring herself to look at Joss and Dan, who was trying to catch her eye. Quickly, she turned back to the stables as fast as she could before anyone could see her. In the safety of Lily's stable, she closed the door behind her and then the tears really began to fall.

CHAPTER EIGHT

Once Lily was settled back in her stable, rugged up against the cold and with Santa, Wilson and Callie in their adjoining boxes, Georgia placed both arms around the little mare's neck, breathing in her scent and feeling her warm and solid against her. Thank goodness for Lily. She had no urge to rush back down to the bottom meadow and watch them finish off the filming. Lily had behaved impeccably so her job was done. And Brodie was right, it *was* just acting. She knew she could get a bit silly over things at times. Joss and Dan's kiss had only been for the camera.

As if in agreement, Lily nudged her and Georgia sighed. "Good girl," she said, rearranging the palomino's warm rugs. "You were brilliant, like always." She hugged Lily tight. "Thank goodness for you," she muttered, suddenly feeling very alone.

There were still a few yard jobs to carry out, due to the fact everyone had rushed down early to watch the filming, so Georgia decided to distract herself by making up that afternoon's hay nets and washing out the breakfast feed bowls. There was something quite peaceful about just hanging out in the yard by herself, compared to all the lights and action in the bottom meadow, and Georgia relished the quiet. Before long, everyone

74

started trooping back up to the yard – Melanie, Sophie and Simon, and Dan, who had changed back into his regular clothes. Seeing Georgia he peeled away from the group and came over to the yard.

"Hey," he said, sounding sheepish.

"Hey!" Georgia said a bit too brightly. She didn't want Dan to know how jealous she was. "You were great!"

Dan reached out and patted Lily's neck thoughtfully. "About the, um, the kiss," he said, looking at the ground. "Brodie said it would work well with the storyline, that's all." He shuffled from side to side. "It was nothing, really."

"It's fine, it's great!" Georgia said quickly, stuffing hay into the brightly coloured nets and avoiding Dan's face, hoping she sounded convincing. There was an awkward pause.

"Well, I'll see you later then," Dan said finally,

brushing Georgia lightly on the arm. "Want to walk back with me?"

Georgia shook her head. "I've still got some jobs to do here," she lied. She was sure Dan was only asking her out of a sense of duty, and besides, she didn't want to talk to him. The filming was over now. She could at last look forward to Olympia and the rest of the Christmas holidays. She had a funny feeling, however, that Joss McCall-Jones wasn't quite out of her life yet...

☆ ☆ ☆

When Georgia was sure Dan would have reached home, and she had said goodbye to Lily, she left the yard on foot. Melanie had offered to drop her off in the 4x4 but Georgia had wanted to be alone for a bit, and use the walk to clear her head. Without Pip, who had been picked up earlier by Georgia's mum, she decided to walk back along the quiet village road instead of cutting over the top meadows that led through Dan's farm.

Trudging along, her wellies crunching the snow underfoot, she was so deep in thought she almost walked straight into the back of an old green Land Rover that was parked in the lay-by between Redgrove Farm and the driveway up to Dan's farm. It was a rickety vehicle, and a brown collie dog with a white patch over one eye yapped and grinned from the back. She smiled, thinking of Dan's sweet dog Hattie. A window wound down as she walked past, making her jump.

"Excuse me." A man, probably in his mid-thirties, leaned his arm on the window. He looked a bit like Dan's dad in dress sense – checked shirt and a wax coat; a typical farmer. Looking around her, suddenly feeling very alone, Georgia paused as the man continued. "I'm looking for Coleman's farm shop."

Feeling relieved, Georgia smiled. "It's up there."

She pointed him towards the lane that led up to Dan's farm and the popular farm shop. Thanking her, the man reversed his Land Rover out of the lay-by and instead of indicating right towards the shop, turned a sharp left and drove off in the opposite direction, the wheels leaving tracks in the dusting of snow.

Staring after him, Georgia shrugged. People were strange. As she passed the entrance to the farm driveway, she paused, thinking how she would normally stop by and hang out with Dan, enjoying the cosy, relaxed friendship they shared. Wavering, she stood for just a minute, before pulling up the hood on her coat and setting off towards home.

☆ ☆ ☆

There were still a couple of days of school left until Georgia, Dan and Emma broke up for the holidays and Georgia couldn't wait – she needed a break. Excited chatter filled the corridors as their school friends discussed their Christmas plans, but mostly everyone wanted to talk to Dan about the filming, and about Joss, and about the fact that she had kissed him. Typically, everyone was especially interested in that bit! Word had quickly spread about his small part in the movie and he was fast becoming a school celebrity. During lunch, Georgia was almost shoved aside by a group of the most popular girls in the year, flanked by Becky Hanbury, who all wanted to know what it had been like. Dan responded in good humour, and the girls giggled and fawned over him, much to Georgia's disgust.

"All OK?" Emma said quietly. She knew Georgia well enough to know she was feeling left out. Georgia nodded, grateful for her best friend. She couldn't wait to get up to the stables once school was over and just concentrate on Lily after the excitement of the last week.

The two friends walked arm in arm towards the bus stop. Emma chatted away about Christmas parties and local gossip, and Georgia listened quietly, glad for the distraction.

"Oh, I forgot to tell you," Emma said as they boarded the bus. "There was a break-in at a farm in Atworth, Dad says. Someone told him in the pub. They stole the sheep; can you imagine?" Emma was referring to a village about seven miles away from Redgrove. Georgia wondered if Dan knew about it. It would worry him if he did. He hadn't mentioned anything to her but perhaps he shared his fears with Joss, now, instead of Georgia.

☆ ☆ ☆

Once the final bell sounded on the last day of the school term, it was with a huge sense of relief that Georgia boarded the school bus. She took her place beside Emma. She and Mum were having dinner in front of the TV that evening and an early night

before the week's countdown to Christmas and Olympia began.

Georgia had a lesson with Will's brother, Jasper, first thing in the morning. He was helping her to prepare for Olympia. While Georgia had been at school, Sophie had been exercising Lily by taking her out on the lead rein when she rode Wilson.

It hadn't snowed since the day of the filming but, glancing at the low sky, Georgia crossed her fingers. She had loved the snow, but hoped it wouldn't return until after they had made the trip to London for Olympia.

Olympia. The mere thought of riding in the famous show sent shivers down Georgia's spine. She thought about the Pony Club trip to Olympia when she was eight years old. And now she was riding there herself! More recently, she had watched Sophie compete there with Callie. She still had to pinch herself when she thought about the fact she had qualified Lily. They had only entered the semi-finals a little while after the Horse of the Year Show, and only then because Jasper had persuaded them to. Georgia hadn't been expecting any sort of placing so it had been amazing when they had been pulled forward to qualify for Olympia. Dan had been there too, and had given Georgia the biggest hug afterwards, practically pulling her off Lily. She smiled at the memory, before frowning. It had obviously meant more to her than to him.

CHAPTER NINE

Jasper was waiting in the yard when Georgia walked up with Pip the next day for her lesson. A former famous show rider, Jasper was a huge hit at the Round Barrow Pony Club. The girls hung on his every word, and the dwindling group of boys hero-worshipped him and kept their Pony Club subscriptions renewed as a result, much to Janey's delight. Georgia had noticed with amusement that Harry was a lot nicer to her now that Jasper and Will kept Santa at Redgrove, and he was always looking for an excuse to get invited over. Harry wasn't so bad. A bit arrogant, and Georgia always noticed how immature he was compared to the hard-working Dan, but all right just the same.

Easy-going, fun and an amazing rider, Jasper was lounging against the arena gate, dressed in dark-green breeches and worn leather half-chaps. His parka jacket was pulled up over his nose. He smiled as Georgia led Lily towards him. She was wearing a wool exercise sheet to keep the chill off and Georgia was bundled up in her old quilted jacket.

"She's looking great," he remarked, running a hand over the palomino's elegant neck as Georgia lightly swung into the saddle. "All set for Olympia?"

Georgia nodded. "Think so," she said in a muffled voice under her scarf. The truth was, unlike with the Horse of the Year Show, she hadn't really had any build-up to the Christmas Championship Show, which had, in turn, had a surprisingly positive effect. Her qualification had been so late and with the end of a busy school term, the arrival of Joss *and* Lily's filming commitment, there hadn't been much time to dwell on it! She was as relaxed as she possibly could be, and as a result her riding had improved hugely – unlike before the Horse of the Year Show, where her nerves had snowballed. Under Jasper's watchful eye, and experience honed from years in the show ring, Lily and Georgia were flourishing.

"Good girl!" Georgia praised Lily over and over as she extended Lily's trot across the arena before walking her round on a long rein at the end of the lesson. For an hour or so she had completely forgotten all about her heartache over Joss and Dan, and thought only about her riding. Ponies were so uncomplicated, she thought. Why couldn't life be as simple?

To her surprise, Dan was waiting in the yard when she walked back to the stables, sitting on a bale of hay in the tack room and playing with Melanie's three terriers, gently tugging a rope toy as they growled with mock ferocity, wagging their stumpy tails. He looked up and smiled when he saw Georgia. "How was your lesson?" he asked.

"Good," Georgia said truthfully. Lily had never felt better. She knew that Dan was still a bit wary about asking how she felt before a show.

"That's nice," Dan said. Then he paused. "Georgia?" he said, hesitating, and Georgia's heart sank. It sounded as though he was about to say something she didn't want to hear.

And she was right. "You know – when we're in London for Olympia?" he said before continuing. "Well, Joss has said we can join her in her exclusive box afterwards, if we want."

Georgia thought about this. It didn't surprise her that Joss was going to be at Olympia; after all, it was a main event on the sporting calendar and it was at the Horse of the Year Show where the actress had spotted Lily for the film. Still, the last thing in the world that she felt like doing was seeing Joss again. She knew Dan was revelling in his film-star moment and didn't want to deny him that, but she had been looking forward to enjoying the show with him, Melanie and Sophie, as normal.

"What do you think?" Dan finished.

"I guess we could," she said, knowing she didn't sound enthusiastic. She had hoped that Dan might have forgotten Joss now that Lily's scenes were over, but they were obviously still very much in contact. Her resolve to concentrate solely on the ponies strengthened. It was all about Lily this Christmas, nothing more, nothing less!

CHAPTER TEN

If Georgia had found it strange driving into Birmingham for the Horse of the Year Show, Olympia was on a completely different level. As the horsebox pulled slowly forward in stop–start traffic, she marvelled at the bustling crowds Christmas shopping in the fading afternoon light. Twinkling fairy lights and fir trees adorned the brightly lit shop windows and the pavements were heaving with shoppers, all weighed down with bags. Winding down her window just a fraction, Georgia felt a little shiver run down her spine as she heard the distant strains of "Silent Night" escaping from the open doorway of a huge department store. She felt the horsebox move slightly as a police car raced past, sirens blaring, and hoped Lily was OK in the back.

Catching her look of apprehension, Melanie smiled. "She's fine, Georgia," she said in a reassuring voice, and Georgia smiled back at her, feeling better. Dan was coming up on an early train the next morning. He didn't have enough money to stay in London overnight and didn't like to leave his sheep for too long, especially as the pet ewe, his favourite, had just given birth to two adorable twin lambs. The recent sheep-rustling case in the local area had also spooked him, despite his dad telling him he was worrying over nothing. But Georgia understood. Secretly she was grateful that he was in London for the least amount of time possible so that he couldn't see Joss so much. Dan was going to watch Georgia ride and then catch the train home as soon as possible so he was back in time to do the animals for the evening. She giggled to herself, imagining Dan on the busy, crowded London trains. He'd probably start chatting to whoever he sat next to about his cows or something!

Knowing how much Dan had to do on the farm, Georgia was especially grateful he was coming to watch. She was trying to ignore the small voice in her head telling her he was coming to see Joss as well. Frowning, she remembered Joss's invitation to come and watch a bit of the show from her private box. It was all very well inviting Georgia, given she had used Lily for the film, but Georgia had the distinct feeling that she was not as welcome as Dan. Ugh! Pulling her knees up to her chest she tried to remind herself that it would hopefully be the last they would see of Joss, but still she couldn't ignore the fact that things had changed between her and Dan. Shutting her eyes, she tried to clear her head of all negative thoughts, and to think about the show tomorrow instead.

✧ ✧ ✧

"We've arrived." Gently, Melanie placed a hand on Georgia's shoulder, rousing her from her slumber. Georgia looked around, startled. The crawling traffic and the warmth of the horsebox had sent her to sleep; she must have been more exhausted than she thought. Next to her, Sophie stretched her long, black-jean-clad legs and yawned, opening her mouth very wide. Sophie had also fallen asleep and was now rubbing her eyes. "Olympia," she grinned sleepily, looking around her. "Now I know it's Christmas!"

Despite the last leg of the journey crawling

through the centre of London and down Kensington High Street, Lily was still calm in the back of the box as they pulled the back ramp down. She held her head high and gazed out into the concrete lorry park, the familiar neighs and sound of metal shoes clip-clopping around mixing with the London buzz of sirens and traffic. Looking around, Georgia smiled shyly as she recognised others riders from the showing scene before her gaze was drawn to a familiar face grinning back at her and waving madly. The girl was holding on to a huge powerful Highland that practically dragged her across the lorry park to snuffle noses with his old friend Lily. It was the beautiful dapple-grey Lachlan, and Alice Smalley was leading him.

"Hey, Georgia!" She high-fived her friend. Georgia was delighted. It was so good to see Alice back competing on the ponies she loved, after her accident.

"How's Secret?" she asked, and Alice laughed.

"Naughty as ever!" she chuckled, tapping her phone to show Georgia endless photos of the little roan pony. Lily's son lived the life of luxury on Josephine Smalley's immaculate showing yard, and her daughter Alice adored him. It was hard to believe he was over a year old now, and even stronger and more handsome than ever, Georgia thought, looking at the photos with pleasure. Suddenly Alice grew wide-eyed and nudged Georgia as she mouthed for her to look behind her.

Turning round, Georgia caught sight of Joss picking her way across the lorry park, flanked as usual by her assistant. She was wearing expensive-looking breeches, which was strange, Georgia thought, considering she wasn't riding.

"Lily!" Joss's tinkly voice carried around the horseboxes. "How *are* you?" She reached out a

94

hand and patted the little mare, who pushed her nose against her arm in greeting. "Oh, look," Joss squealed. "She remembers me!" Then, noticing a young girl hovering nearby with a phone, she gave a megawatt grin, turning Lily around so she was facing the screen. "Of course you can have a photo!"

Georgia felt the familiar bubble of jealousy rise up again as she was virtually pushed out of the way. Lily was *her* pony! Catching Sophie's eye, she felt relieved as her friend pulled a face and giggled, realising the young girl only wanted a photo of Lily, and not Joss. Once the girl had gone, Joss handed Lily's lead rope back to Georgia, and fell in step with the group as they made their way to the stabling area.

"What's with the breeches?" Sophie enquired curiously. "Are you riding?"

"I've just come from my lesson," Joss explained.

"In Hyde Park," she added with a flourish. Then when Georgia looked at her blankly, she laughed. "There's a famous stables there, silly. And I'll let you into a secret – I'm going to have my very own pony to keep there soon!"

"Really?" Georgia couldn't help but raise an eyebrow. Joss loved ponies, that was clear to see, but she didn't seem to know much about looking after one. Still, she reasoned, she was obviously doing pretty well as an actress, so maybe soon she would be able to employ a fleet of grooms!

"So," Joss continued, linking an arm with Georgia as she entered the stable area. Melanie was sorting out some bits in the lorry and Sophie had stopped to speak to an old showing friend. "The pony I'm going to buy is right here! He's competing tomorrow, like you. I've already bought him!" Georgia just gaped at her. It was a different world really, being able to buy a pony just like that, and a top-class show pony as well. Georgia smiled weakly.

"You must come and see him as soon as the show's over. You'll love him, Georgia," Joss said, waving goodbye. "A palomino, like Lily. I wanted one just like her!"

CHAPTER ELEVEN

If Georgia was curious about the pony Joss had bought, she didn't really have much time to think about it. There was so much to do, including setting up Lily's stable and lugging her trunk full of tack and grooming kits across what seemed like miles of concrete lorry park. Sophie was in her element, racing around saying hi to the other riders. She still rode Wilson when home for the holidays but rarely competed any more and was enjoying not having the pressure of riding in the ring herself. Georgia was always grateful when Sophie came along to her shows; she was experienced and kind, just like Melanie.

Melanie was as calm as ever. Placing a hand on Georgia's shoulder, she smiled. "Ready for this?" she asked kindly, and Georgia nodded, really meaning it. She still couldn't believe she was competing at the famous Christmas show. Later on, warming up in her allocated time slot she relaxed as Lily paid no attention to the glitzy decorations hanging in the arena, ignoring some of the ponies who sidestepped past, eyes bulging, necks quivering as they took in the huge atmosphere and the echoes of the vast exhibition centre.

Remembering what Joss had told her, she curiously scanned some of the ponies as she warmed down on a loose rein, trying to guess which one she had bought. There was a pretty Welsh Section A mare and a solid Shetland stallion, both palomino, but Georgia guessed they would be too small, even for the tiny Joss. Then suddenly, out of the corner of her eye, she noticed a magnificent Welsh Section D cob high-stepping into the arena. The pony was at the top end of its height range and oozed presence and fire. Georgia watched as it pushed into a powerful extended trot. It was obviously strong and the girl riding was struggling to control its enthusiasm. As the pony thundered past Georgia, she practically felt the ground shake, like an earthquake. She recognised the girl on the palomino as a show rider who made a living riding ponies on behalf of professional yards, and she was probably in her early twenties. Even she was struggling with the pony! But there was no time to speculate. After Melanie was satisfied that Lily was happy and confident with her new surroundings, it was time to settle her into her temporary stable, which Sophie had decorated with gold tinsel around the door.

"Our Olympia tradition." She winked at Georgia and for the millionth time Georgia thought how lucky she was that Redgrove had become her second home.

✧ ✧ ✧

Later, curled up in her bed in the hotel room she was sharing with Sophie, Georgia checked her phone. Good-luck texts from Emma, who was coming on the Pony Club coach early the next morning, and Dan, letting her know he would make it in time for her class. He still had to work in the morning, which was why his dad had agreed to drop him at the train station, so he could get to London as fast as he could. The text had only just been sent, so quickly she replied:

Can't wait to see you tomorrow x

But nothing came back. Sighing, she put her phone on the little table beside her bed and, putting a pillow over her head to block out the sound of the London traffic, drifted into a deep sleep.

☆ ☆ ☆

Cantering around the warm-up area at six the next morning, Georgia reflected on just how surreal everything was. Lily was as relaxed as ever as Georgia concentrated on her transitions, running through her individual show under Melanie's watchful eye. Checking her watch, Georgia hoped that Dan had caught his early train. If he had, he should just make it in time for the class. Unlike at the Horse of the Year Show when he had come into the ring as official groom, Melanie was going to be carrying out that duty, just in case the train was delayed and to stop Georgia fretting. Georgia was just glad Dan was coming to watch, and hoped he would find his seat OK, as he wouldn't be able to watch from the horse area without an official badge. It would be strange without him by her side.

✩ ✪ ✩

"Breakfast?" Sophie grinned as Georgia untacked Lily back in her stable. She wasn't that nervous now she had ridden Lily in the warm-up, but she felt faintly sick – the kind of sick you feel when you have to get up really early to go on holiday. Sophie was munching her way through an enormous bacon roll, slathered in ketchup. The smell, normally Georgia's favourite, made her senses reel and she felt a wave of nausea. She shook her head, her mouth clamped together, and Sophie laughed. "For once I can relax and watch!" she said cheerfully. "I'll buy you loads of food after your class. You'll need it by then!"

✩ ✬ ✩

Sophie was right. Georgia felt her tummy growl as she mounted Lily, ready to take her to the main arena. Oh well, it was too late now. She would just have to wait until after the riding was done. Reaching down, she gave Lily a pat with her gloved hand, remembering her and Melanie's trip to buy them before the Horse of the Year Show. They had brought her luck then. Could they do the same now? The commentator was whipping the crowd into a frenzy of excitement and the ponies in front of Georgia jigged with pent-up nerves as the stewards called the riders forward.

The Exmoors, Dartmoors and Shetlands had already been in for their preliminary judging. It was now the turn of the Welsh ponies before the large breeds. Then they would all be back later on for the placing. It was a format that Georgia knew like the back of her hand, having watched Sophie compete in the past.

"Good luck!"

Turning round, Georgia grinned as she heard a familiar voice. Will and his brother Jasper were waving at her, thumbs aloft. She had no idea how they had managed to sneak into the horse area but guessed it was because Jasper had been a famous rider. However they had done it, Georgia was delighted to see them.

The actual show part was much the same as every other show Georgia had done – a go-round with the other ponies, an individual show and a trot-up in front of the confirmation judge. The same as every show bar the enormous crowds and Christmas decorations everywhere, and the fact they were cantering around one of the most famous equestrian arenas in the world! Georgia tried not to think too hard about that, instead concentrating on showing Lily off perfectly. Her now-trademark extended trot got a huge cheer, much to Georgia's delight, and the rest of the show went perfectly, even her weak spot, the right canter lead. Lily simply shone under the arena lights. It seemed the bigger the crowd, the better her performance. Georgia crossed her fingers and hoped that Dan had managed to find his seat and was watching, knowing she had just ridden the best show she had ever performed. Melanie obviously felt the same and was grinning from ear to ear as the pair rode out of the arena, taking hold of Lily's bridle, tears of happiness threatening to spill over. Mel loved the little palomino as much as Georgia did!

"Wonderful, super, perfect," she enthused tearfully, patting her over and over. Then, as Georgia dismounted, Mel took one look at her pale face and ordered her towards the food stalls to grab some breakfast before the mounted prize-giving.

Protesting, Georgia tried to assure her that she was fine, but Melanie insisted that she and Sophie would look after Lily. Georgia decided to see if Dan had arrived, and if she could sneak him into the horse area somehow, like Jasper and Will. It didn't feel the same without him there. She decided to go and find his seat, which she knew was one of the lower-priced tickets near the food hall. Weaving in and out of the bustling crowds, heading towards the shopping village, she was just about to turn into the section where his seat was located when her eye was drawn to a familiar figure sitting in one of the many cafes on the ringside. He was laughing, head close to a strikingly pretty girl. She had her hand on his arm, throwing her head back in a fit of giggles as they shared a joke. Joss and Dan.

Georgia felt her heart sink to the bottom of her boots, and suddenly decided she didn't want to be anywhere near them. Maybe they wouldn't notice her go. Turning back, she was ready to disappear into the crowds and slink back to the comfort of Lily when she heard her name being called. It was Joss and she was waving madly at Georgia. Her cheeks flushing, Georgia had no choice but to head over. Dan looked a little sheepish, pulling his arm away from Joss's grasp. "Hey, G," he smiled at his friend. "How did it go?"

"Good." Georgia looked questioningly at Dan, and he held his hands up.

"Sorry, Georgia, my train got delayed. I couldn't work out the tube and I couldn't exactly ring you, but luckily Joss came to my rescue."

Joss beamed at this. "London's easy for me," she said in her tinkly voice. "It was *so* funny seeing you trying to work that ticket barrier, Dan!"

The two collapsed into laughter again, chatting about some earlier shared experience, as Georgia sat awkwardly, feeling like a third wheel. She suddenly found she had totally lost her appetite. Smiling weakly, she stood up.

"Well," she said turning back. "I'd better get on with things; the prize-giving is soon."

"I'll be watching," Dan said loyally. "And, Georgia … I'm really sorry I missed your show."

He did sound sincere, and Georgia was just about to answer when Joss beamed. "I'll come and find you at the stables later; I'd like to see my new horse. Also, I've got something exciting to tell you!"

Scurrying back to the stables, all thoughts of food forgotten, Georgia wondered what she meant. Try as she might, she couldn't get the image of Joss and Dan giggling together out of her mind.

CHAPTER TWELVE

There wasn't time for Georgia to think about her wounded feelings. The break between the judging and the prize-giving had flown by, broken up with a display from a horsey stunt team that had the huge Olympia crowds whooping and cheering in excitement. All too soon, Georgia needed to remount for the final results. Given the formality of the occasion, she was wearing Sophie's old navy jacket and a snow-white stock, rather than her normal tweed and tie. Sophie had pinned her mass of blonde hair into a bun, and her lucky silver stock pin sparkled. Melanie stepped back and looked at Georgia as she pulled her gloves on before mounting.

"My," she said proudly. "Aren't you looking grown up!"

Georgia smiled, thinking of the first time her mum had taken her over to Redgrove. In those days it had been a dream just to be near ponies, and now here she was, riding in one of the most famous shows in the country. If Dan really did like Joss ... at least she still had Lily and the other ponies.

Sophie pulled out a compact mirror from her handbag and held it up so Georgia could see her reflection. With her blonde waves pinned tightly back and the snow-white stock setting off her pale skin, she hardly dared think it, but she looked *sophisticated*. With her confidence slightly boosted, she gathered up her reins, her head held high.

As Georgia trotted Lily into the main arena behind the other Section Bs, the atmosphere was crackling with electricity. The stands were now completely full of spectators, all waiting excitedly for the results. As Georgia trotted down the long side of the arena, concentrating on keeping Lily light between her hands and focused, her eye was drawn to the boxes above the seating area. There was some particularly enthusiastic waving and cheering coming from one box and, looking up, Georgia saw Emma and Dan clapping wildly. Her heart leapt for one moment, before she realised Joss was nestled in beside them, grinning up at Dan and not watching the ponies at all. Georgia gritted her teeth. *Concentrate*, she told herself sternly.

This was possibly the biggest moment of her riding career and she didn't want to be distracted! Thank goodness for Lily, she thought, giving the little mare a scratch on her withers as she took her place in the line-up.

The ponies were called out in reverse order from tenth place, with the best of breeds announced as they went. Alice Smalley whooped with delight as she and Lachlan were placed seventh.

Georgia grinned at her. Alice was so brave to be riding again after her accident, let alone competing at the top level, and the cheers from the crowd reflected that. As the commentator, a man in a tuxedo holding a microphone, neared the final three places, Georgia started to feel her excitement grow as she realised the best of breed for the Welsh Section B still hadn't been announced. That meant a Section B had to be in the top three. When the name of the third-placed pony – a handsome Dartmoor stallion – was announced, Georgia started to hold her breath. Melanie had told her that Lily had looked the best she had ever looked, but to win at Olympia? Georgia hardly dared breathe. The reserve champion went to the most gorgeous grey Connemara whose rider leaned forward to hug her pony over and over again. There was a dramatic pause before the first place was announced. "And our Olympia champion this year goes to … Carlamu Lily and Miss Georgia Black!"

Time seemed to stand still. Georgia felt the blood rush to her ears and her heart felt as though it might burst out of her chest. The stands erupted, everyone cheering. The little palomino was a popular winner and it was all Georgia could do to stay mounted as she hugged Lily tightly, tears pouring down her cheeks. She had known Lily was special from the moment she first saw her on the wet hillside in Wales, and now she was proving it to the whole equestrian world. As Georgia walked Lily forward to receive her championship rosette and sash, and to pose for the hundreds of cameras, she didn't think the moment could ever be topped. It was only after she completed her lap of honour, finishing with a gallop under a spotlight, that she remembered her friends watching. Glancing up at the box where Dan and Joss sat, now joined by Will and Jasper, she felt her stomach flip as she saw Joss had her arms firmly wrapped around Dan.

An ecstatic, tearful Melanie met her as she trotted back out of the arena. Melanie was so overcome with emotion that she could hardly speak at first. She just hugged both Lily and Georgia over and over. Sophie was equally excited. Georgia could have burst with pride! Putting Dan and Joss firmly out of her mind, she concentrated instead on untacking Lily and rugging her up before she got cold in the chill of the backstage area. People were stopping to congratulate her every minute, and she felt her cheeks might start to ache with all the smiling she was doing. It would be a very happy lorry heading back to Redgrove that evening.

CHAPTER THIRTEEN

Georgia's celebrations were interrupted by Emma, who, squealing with delight, flung her arms around her friend before hugging Lily.

"Oh my goodness, Georgia, that was *amazing*!" Emma was jumping up and down in excitement.

"Thanks," Georgia mumbled, unable to muster any more than one word in her emotional state. She felt a little overwhelmed all of a sudden – the early morning, lack of food and now the win were catching up with her and making her feel a little unsteady on her feet. Following Emma were Dan and Joss. Dan did look really pleased but Georgia couldn't help but notice that Joss was by his side, staring adoringly up at Dan.

She's clinging to him like a limpet, she thought, and then she stopped herself. She knew she was being unkind.

"Well done, G," Dan said warmly, and Georgia thanked him, avoiding his eye.

"You can meet my new pony now!" Joss trilled. "He was the one who was fifth!"

Thinking back, Georgia realised the pony Joss meant was indeed the strong-looking Welsh in the warm-up. She frowned. Joss was a novice rider, and the pony, whose name she quickly learned was Topper, looked a real handful. She just hoped Joss would have help on a good yard. However,

Joss had further, unexpected news that totally deflated Georgia.

"Soooo," she said batting her long eyelashes. "My riding school in Hyde Park can't take him until the new year. And I'm filming near Redgrove up until Christmas Eve anyway, then going back to London to see my family. So…"

Georgia stared at her. She had a sudden horrible feeling she knew what Joss was about to say, and braced herself. Joss went on to explain that her new pony was being sent to Redgrove that evening and was to be kept at Seven Birches, an exclusive livery yard, over the Christmas period. It was only five minutes' walk from Dan's farm, Georgia thought.

No wonder Joss looked so pleased with herself. Turning back to Lily so Dan wouldn't see the hurt that had crossed her face she mumbled a reply, trying to sound happy. Truthfully, she *was* worried that the pony Joss had bought was far too much for her, and despite being the same colour as Lily, was nothing like her in temperament. But seeing Joss gazing up at Dan, she decided not to say anything. Despite having just won the biggest show of her life, Georgia felt as though the sun had gone behind a cloud. Shaking all thoughts of Dan and Joss from her mind she gave Lily a big hug instead. Today was all about her little mare, and she was the only one that mattered.

When Lily was finally settled back into her stable, and the stream of well-wishers had drifted away, Georgia remembered Joss's invitation to watch the rest of the show from her private box. She got the impression that although Sophie was on her side when it came to Joss, she was keen to take full advantage of the offer! Melanie wanted Lily to settle for an hour or so with her feed before driving home, so there was time to spare.

"Come on." Sophie practically dragged her friend down the aisles to the boxes, passing hundreds of excited pony-mad girls and boys on the way. Georgia soon found herself in a plush box overlooking the whole arena. Sophie had been right; there was something quite magical about watching the show from the highest point. The showjumping was finishing up in the arena below, and the mounted prize-giving was underway to rapturous applause as the prize-winners, including three Whitakers, cantered their big warmbloods around the arena. As the team of helpers scurried around, clearing the vast space ready for the Christmas parade, the lights dimmed and excitement rippled through the crowd. Glancing over, Georgia caught Dan's eye. She desperately wanted to go and sit next to him, to enjoy the carols and the horses and the arrival of Father Christmas on a sleigh pulled by the most beautiful chestnut, but the presence of Joss hovering right beside him kept her back.

Joss smiled at her, but Georgia noticed her eyes were cold and her smile completely insincere. Her expression clearly said "back off". Sitting down beside Sophie, Georgia felt her eyes swim with tears, barely able to concentrate on the happy scene below her.

As the crowd erupted into the chorus of "The First Noel" she thought her heart might break and, making her excuses, ran out of the box and straight back to the stables where she slumped down next to her beloved pony as the Christmas cheer continued without her. It seemed that no one, not even Emma, had noticed her leave. It had been the happiest day of Georgia's life, winning at Olympia, but also one of the worst. How was that even possible, she thought, shaking her head in despair. She knew it was partly her own fault –

she had always expected Dan to just be there. And now he didn't know, might not *ever* know, just how much he meant to her.

☆ ☆ ☆

"You're quiet." Melanie turned to Georgia as the dark-green lorry pulled out of a service station and back on to the motorway. Sophie was asleep beside them, her blonde and pink hair tucked into her grey hood. Lily had been happily eating her hay when Georgia had gone to check on her, but Georgia would be glad to get her home and into her own stable.

"Just tired," Georgia said truthfully. It had been the most emotional, amazing day and she felt totally drained. After coming to say goodbye, and some awkward small talk, Dan had left to catch his train home, and Joss had skipped off beside him. Georgia was trying to put Dan out of her mind completely.

"You did brilliantly today, Georgia, you know," Melanie continued, looking thoughtful. "We always knew Lily was a great pony, but it's all been down to you – you put the work in. It's hard to know what she can do next from here really."

Georgia felt herself blush at the compliment. Melanie was right – eleven-year-old Lily came from a superior line of Welsh ponies, but she had needed to learn to trust people again after her treatment at the hands of her former rider. Georgia wondered what next year would hold for them. Perhaps she could concentrate on something entirely different – dressage, maybe.

As they passed the sign welcoming them into Redgrove, Georgia stretched and unfolded her stiff, aching legs. The roads were silent and a heavy frost was already clinging to the fields, swathing them in silver, eerie in the moonlight. Suddenly Melanie cursed under her breath as a lorry coming in the other direction forced the horsebox into the side of the road, jolting Sophie awake. Bringing the lorry to a stop as smoothly as she could manage, Melanie held up her hand to the driver, as if to ask him what he was thinking. The driver of the other lorry, a ramshackle silver vehicle, drove straight past without even acknowledging Melanie, who frowned.

"Didn't look like any of the farmers from around here," she muttered, but it was soon forgotten as they drove up the Redgrove Farm drive where Wilson, Callie and Santa whinnied with pleasure at seeing Lily again. To Georgia's delight, her mum was waiting in the yard. Unable to travel up to Olympia because of a work deadline, she had instead pinned a congratulations banner to Lily's stable door, and hugged her daughter over and over as she led an equally tired Lily off the horsebox. After all the excitement of the last twenty-four hours, Georgia was just grateful to see her mum and a bit of normality. It had been a whirlwind December with the arrival of Joss, and the filming, and Olympia. All Georgia wanted to do now was to curl up in her pyjamas and show her mum the photos from the show … to relive her winning performance over and over again!

CHAPTER FOURTEEN

"Here's the Christmas hero!" Will grinned at Georgia as she opened the gates to the yard the next morning. It was a perfect winter's day, crisp and cold, with a sun so bright that Georgia had considered wearing sunglasses. She reflected on the fact that when she had first met Will she would have assumed he was being sarcastic or patronising, but there was only warmth in his voice now. She smiled, patting Lily, who eagerly thrust her nose into her palm. Despite Georgia's own exhaustion, she had barely slept last night, and had just replayed the winning moment in her head a hundred times. Adrenalin had been surging through her body until the early hours and she had flicked endlessly through the photos that Sophie had taken on her phone. It still felt surreal. But there was a niggling thorn in the back of her mind, no matter how much she tried to block it out… Dan.

It was obvious that Dan fancied Joss, and vice versa. Miserably, Georgia recounted all the times that Dan had told her why he preferred her to other girls – she was hard-working, and loved animals and the outdoors. But now Joss had come along, and not only did she like ponies as well, but she was a super-glossy version of a normal girl, and there was no way Georgia could compete. She realised that for the last year and a half, she and Dan had never really spoken about their relationship, preferring the easy friendship that came so naturally to them. But now someone else was in the picture and Georgia couldn't do anything about it. She may be the best show pony rider in the country at that present moment, but this was one competition she couldn't win!

"Earth to Georgia." Will waved a hand in front of her face, jolting her back to reality. Shaking her head, she smiled weakly, trying to erase the image of Dan and Joss leaving Olympia from her mind.

"Sorry, Will," she said, collecting up Lily's head collar, ready to turn the little mare out for a well-deserved rest.

"I was just saying about the mock hunt," Will explained. "How many people are coming... Georgia, are you all right?"

Will was really looking at her now, clearly

noticing her sad expression and the dark circles under her eyes.

Georgia nodded her head. If she tried to explain about Dan, she was afraid she might cry. "I'm just really tired," she mumbled. "It's been a busy month."

Seemingly satisfied with her reply, Will patted her on the shoulder and then carried on his enthusiastic chatter about the mock hunt.

Nodding and smiling in the right places, Georgia tried to concentrate on what he was saying but inside she felt as though her heart was breaking in two.

Still, at least the ponies were a distraction. Long after Will had gone home for the morning, Georgia stayed around the yard, finding little jobs to do or just spending time with the four ponies, particularly Lily, who didn't seem to mind eating her hay with Georgia's arm draped over her neck. Melanie was out Christmas shopping with Sophie and Simon, and the yard was peaceful and quiet.

Georgia decided to keep herself busy; she would make a start on mucking out the fields, which was usually a joint effort between her, Will and Melanie. But without Dan's farm to go and hang out at, and wanting to avoid twenty questions from Emma, Georgia decided it was the better alternative.

Pushing a wheelbarrow towards the top meadow, which overlooked the valley, she tried not to look at the frosty fields that sloped down towards Dan's farm. Concentrating instead on the job in hand, she slowly pushed the wheelbarrow back and forth as she cleared the field. Stopping by the bare hawthorn hedge overlooking the whole valley, she paused, catching her breath. No wonder she was always hungry – horses were hard work!

Picking up the wheelbarrow handles, she was

just about to set off down the hill back towards the yard when an excited yap caught her attention. Turning eastwards, she saw a collie dog crouching low in the meadow below. There was a public footpath that snaked along the fields towards Dan's farm but the dog was way off-path. Georgia looked harder at the little dog, who seemed familiar. She knew she had seen the dog before – Georgia always remembered animals. Then she realised – it was the same little collie that had been grinning at her from the back of the old Land Rover, the day she had walked home from Redgrove after Lily's filming.

There was a long, low whistle and the dog launched forward into a long, graceful stride, catching up with a figure skirting the edge of the woods. He bent forward to pat the collie before continuing on his way. For just one second, as the man stood back up, he looked straight up at

Georgia. She couldn't explain it, but a chill ran through her. Hurriedly dragging the full wheelbarrow behind her, she tripped her way back down the hill and into the safe warmth of the tack room. Thinking about it later that afternoon, when she had finished tidying the yard, she supposed she ought to let Dan know there had been a walker and dog straying off the footpath. It wasn't ideal with the lambs around.

Hesitating, she thought about going to visit Dan as she often did when she had finished at Redgrove. She decided there was no reason why she shouldn't. Dan was still her friend. It was her fault that she had read more into it! And Georgia knew she should notify him if she ever noticed anything suspicious surrounding the farm.

Setting off for home back across the top field she was soon heading up the drive to the farm, greeting Hattie and the tame chickens on the way.

Rounding the corner to the bungalow, she stopped in her tracks as a handsome palomino head popped out of the little stable next to the sheep barn. *Secret's* stable.

It was Joss's new pony, but what was he doing here? Looking around, Georgia felt her blood freeze as she caught sight of Joss exiting the farm shop with Dan, throwing back her head and laughing as Ben, his older brother, joined them. She smiled when she caught sight of Georgia: a cool, smug smile.

"Oh hi, Georgia!" she waved, fastening her riding hat back on her head.

"Hi," Georgia muttered in reply, glancing at Dan.

"Joss got a bit lost getting back to her yard," Dan explained. "She stopped here so I could give her directions."

Georgia raised an eyebrow. Seven Birches was less than a mile away, and on a straight road. She

134

doubted very much that Joss had managed to get lost!

"And I was so cold, Dan invited me to the shop for a hot chocolate!" Joss beamed, leading Topper back out of his stable and looking *very* pleased with herself.

It was the final straw for Georgia. That was her and Dan's special thing, not his and Joss's. She felt like stamping her feet like a toddler but instead she stared coolly at Joss.

Joss was still smiling as she tried to remount the big Section D. He was obviously wound up from stopping in the strange stable and wouldn't stand still as she hopped around, trying to get her foot in the stirrup.

Georgia knew she should step forward to get hold of the pony's bridle and calm him, and to hold the other stirrup down, but she was so upset that she stood aside, while Dan and Ben attempted to hold the pony still. Georgia thought how Topper was far too powerful for an inexperienced rider like Joss, and what a stupid idea it was trying to ride him the day after he arrived at a new yard, but she kept her mouth shut. It wasn't her problem, and she didn't exactly feel like advising Joss. Once they had clattered down the drive, the pony making a beeline for Seven Birches, Dan turned to Georgia.

"Sorry, G," he said, his face reddening. "She just turned up."

"I bet," Georgia said sharply. Making an excuse, not wanting to hang around a minute later, she strode back down the drive, all thoughts of the wandering dog walker forgotten.

CHAPTER FIFTEEN

As Georgia lay in bed early on Christmas Eve morning, one arm around Pip, who wriggled and squirmed in her sleep, she reflected on how much she had achieved over the past year. Her time on a showing yard in the spring, and her decision to gift Lily's foal, Secret, to Alice had been a huge part of it. Then qualifying Lily for both the Horse of the Year Show *and* Olympia had been a total dream come true, topped only by actually winning at Olympia. She should have been feeling on top of the world, but instead she wanted to scream out loud. Why hadn't she told Dan how she felt about him when she had the chance?

Sighing and flinging off her duvet cover, she stood in her bare feet and surveyed the garden in the half-light. There were still patches of snow lying in the shade, but the sun was just starting to rise in the east, casting a pink glow over the trees. It looked bitterly cold though, and Georgia decided to put her thermal leggings on under her jodhpurs. At least her tweed coat was warm, as well as smart. Her mum, still in her dressing gown, was already in the kitchen, adding honey to a bowl of porridge.

"Thought you would need something warm before riding." She smiled at her daughter and Georgia ate it gratefully, as her mum sat next to her and stroked Ralphy, their tabby cat, who lay lazily across the table. "Are all your friends going to the mock hunt today?" Mrs Black asked, and Georgia paused between mouthfuls, nodding.

"Yes. Sophie, and Will, and Harry…" Well, he sort of counted as a friend now. Her mum raised an eyebrow. "Dan not going?" she said as casually as possible, noticing Georgia reddening.

"Think so," she mumbled. "When he's finished doing the farm."

Seeing Georgia's downcast face, her mum clearly decided not to question further, but instead busied herself packing a flask of hot tea, as she was coming to watch the mock hunt.

When Georgia got to Redgrove, Sophie was waiting in the yard for her. Sophie couldn't decide if she was more excited about riding Wilson in the mock hunt or the Pony Club party she was also going to later, but, either way, she was bubbling with enthusiasm as she and Georgia mucked out the ponies. Georgia smiled, thinking that Sophie felt like the big sister she'd never had! Callie, the only pony not going to the meet, watched with interest as the girls, who were soon joined by Will, set to work preparing the ponies.

Lily, a pure Section B, didn't need to be plaited but was turned out as a true native instead, so Georgia took her time combing out her creamy mane and body-brushing her until she shone. A lick of hoof oil set off her dainty feet.

When all three ponies were finally ready, Santa's and Wilson's dark-brown manes neatly plaited and all three ponies gleaming, the trio tacked up and mounted. They made a breathtaking sight as they clattered three abreast down the Redgrove drive. Melanie and Simon came round to the front of the house to wave them off and take pictures.

"Have fun!" Melanie called out proudly. "Have

you all got your mobiles, in case I need to collect you?"

"Yes," chorused all three as the ponies jigged about, sensing they were off somewhere exciting, rather than just a normal hack.

They made a fantastic sight trotting through the village of Redgrove, saying good morning to dog walkers and thanking cars as they passed. For the first time in a few days, Georgia began to feel a little better. Lily was full of beans, pinging down the road beside the two bigger ponies. Melanie had been right, a change from showing would do Lily the world of good, and taking her mind off Dan had made Georgia feel better already.

☆ ☆ ☆

The mock hunt meet was being held at an old manor house on the outskirts of Redgrove, owned by the former District Commissioner of the Round Barrow Pony Club.

"She's even scarier than Janey!" Sophie had giggled.

Jasper, relishing his new role as Pony Club instructor, had managed to charm the elderly couple into holding the mock hunt on their land. From the number of horseboxes and trailers in the field, he had done a brilliant job in encouraging all the young riders in the area to attend, including some from rival pony clubs, all full of chattering excitement about the canter ahead and the party afterwards.

Georgia had tried to convince Emma to come along as well and ride the cob pony from the riding school she borrowed from time to time, but she had cheerfully declined, preferring to sit and watch Christmas films by the fire instead. Not even the prospect of Will riding alongside her could tempt her out today, although she had promised Georgia she would come to the party afterwards.

Georgia glanced at the low purple-tinged sky that threatened snow, knowing that she would still rather be out on Lily than by a warm fire, even if her feet were already frozen inside her riding boots! Lily danced a little from side to side, tossing her head as she took in the crowd of ponies and riders in front of her. The atmosphere was affecting all of the Redgrove ponies, even steady old Wilson, who flared his nostrils in excitement, particularly when the huntsman, mounted on a beautiful bay cob, rode past flanked by a pack of baying tan and black hounds who cavorted and skipped, rolling joyfully on the wet grass.

Jasper was now talking to one of the senior Pony Clubbers who was one of the fastest cross-country runners in the county. Georgia watched with interest as he stretched before setting off at a fast pace across the open parkland surrounding the manor house and disappearing into the woods beyond. She knew they were going to be following his trail, after giving him a head start.

Lily, now famous among the Pony Club members after her Olympia win, was receiving lots of pats from the gathered crowd. Scanning the hordes of people, Georgia caught sight of her mum, waving proudly, and smiled. Mrs Black was completely unhorsey but supported Georgia all the way and adored Lily.

"Uh-oh, look to your left," Will suddenly hissed in her ear, and Georgia turned, her jaw dropping at the sight of Joss clattering up the drive on Topper, who looked thoroughly overexcited and whose big neck was already lathered in white foam. Joss was clinging on to a neck strap, but still somehow managed to look serene and elegant.

Trailing behind on foot was Dan. He waved at the group and walked over to join them.

"Honestly," Will scoffed while they were still

144

out of earshot. "That girl hasn't got the message yet, has she?"

"What message?" Georgia looked straight at Will, and he laughed.

"Oh come off it, Georgia, she's mad about Dan, but—" He didn't get to finish his sentence as Joss and Topper were suddenly in the middle of the group, the big pony causing an almighty commotion among the Redgrove ponies as he danced from side to side, banging into them and tossing his big, golden handsome head in the air.

"Top-per!" Joss sounded slightly breathless and nervous as she struggled to control the Welsh cob. Her inexperience was showing on her new pony.

"I didn't think you'd be here today," Georgia frowned, sounding more hostile than she had intended. Joss laughed and then turned pale as Topper plunged forward.

"I'm not going back to my family in London

until tonight," she explained. "Dan told me about this mock hunt and I thought it would be fun!" She smiled down at Dan, who had now caught up with the group. "He's been *so* kind to me during my stay here."

Georgia noticed that Dan reddened slightly at this remark and turned to look at Georgia. But just then the huntsman signalled for the young riders to follow him through the gate and out into the parkland beyond the manor house. The ponies, ears pricked and adrenalin pumping through their veins, surged forward eagerly. The Pony Club Christmas Eve Mock Hunt was underway!

CHAPTER SIXTEEN

Glancing behind her as Lily set off at a floating trot alongside the other ponies, Georgia saw Dan, who she knew was helping to man the horsebox field for the rest of the afternoon. She wondered what Will had been about to say about Joss. She must remember to ask him about it later. For now though, she had to concentrate on holding Lily back. The excitement of being out in the open with at least thirty other ponies trotting alongside had wound Lily up slightly and she felt as fresh as she had ever felt!

Georgia was glad Lily was behaving; one or two of the Pony Club members had already turned back, their ponies completely out of control. Jasper, at the front of the group, was keeping the field at a steady pace. Either side of Georgia, Wilson and Santa cantered with their ears pricked forwards, Sophie and Will grinning from ear to ear. This was what riding was all about, Georgia thought to herself. Out in the open countryside with her friends by her side. If only Joss hadn't turned up it would have been perfect.

Topper, slightly behind the group, was sidestepping, shaking his head in frustration at not being allowed to gallop free. He looked a real handful, and for a moment Georgia wondered if she should hang back and check Joss was coping with the powerful gelding. Then, remembering how annoyed she was at Joss, Georgia kept on trotting forward. They were soon out in the rolling parkland beyond the manor house, and the field set off in a controlled canter. As the cold air whipped past Georgia's face, causing her eyes to sting and her cheeks to numb with the chill, she laughed out loud. Will had been totally right – Lily was enjoying herself immensely, and after all of her schooling and shows it was a real treat to allow her to have her head, her long elegant strides eating up the parkland.

"Oh … oh, help!" She suddenly heard a cry from behind her as the field came to a stop at the top of the valley.

Turning round, Georgia noticed Topper leap into the air like a salmon, Joss clinging with all her strength to his pale mane and neck strap.

"All OK?" Will shouted back, and Joss laughed,

but Georgia noticed the nervous undertone.

"Fine!" Joss replied. "He's just a bit spirited!"

Turning to Georgia, Will said in a low voice, "Do you think I should hack back home with her?" Georgia shrugged. If Joss wanted to be out on the big gelding, it was her choice. Still, Georgia wrestled with her conscience – her instinct was always to help a fellow rider.

But before Will could make a decision the field were off again, streaming over the valley and popping over the cross-country fences as they went. Georgia felt that Lily had never been more powerful and spirited as Georgia took the weight off her saddle, folding forward like an event rider as she kept a light contact with Lily's mouth. Now that the initial excitement had worn off, Lily had settled and pony and rider were in perfect sync. Will had caught up with Jasper, and the two brothers were way out in front – Santa and the iron-grey pony Jasper was riding in perfect stride with each other. Looking around, Georgia noticed she had lost Sophie as well. Sophie had hung back with Wilson and an old Pony Club friend and the two were gossiping merrily, loping along at a good pace. It was only Georgia and Joss together, and Georgia shouted angrily as Topper ploughed into Lily, Joss struggling to control him.

After the first hour of cantering and jumping, the field dwindled and was now separated into little pockets of riders. Jasper, noticing the snow clouds drawing in, had announced that they would call it a day after they had reached the woods beyond the valley. Everyone had had a brilliant ride, but he didn't want the Pony Club members to have to hack back in the snow.

As Topper drew up beside Lily, Georgia noticed that although the rest of the ponies had settled, Topper seemed even stronger, and naughtier with it. He was obviously fed up and Joss was still clinging on to the neck strap as if her life depended on it. Georgia opened her mouth to tell Joss to relax and sit up straight but before she could say anything, Topper spun his powerful back legs round and, whipping the reins from Joss's hands, half reared. He bolted back down the valley, the ground thudding as he lengthened his stride, the distance between him and the rest of the riders increasing. Panicked, Georgia realised with horror that as she was standing near the back of the group, nobody else had noticed Topper bolt.

For a fleeting second she was torn. Joss had taken Dan away from her. Still, she couldn't leave her in trouble, or risk the handsome gelding being injured. Wheeling Lily round, she nudged her forward with her heels and set off at a fast canter after Topper. Her logical brain told her that Topper wouldn't want to leave the ponies for long and would soon stop. She could ride with Joss back to Jasper and get him to accompany them home.

But as they cantered further and further away, she realised Topper had other ideas and was still bolting ahead of them. They had reached the huge open field now, overlooking the village of Redgrove, and both ponies had left the rest of the Pony Club far behind them. Georgia could hear Joss's screaming above the wind and realised the girl was seriously scared. The big powerful pony clearly had no intention of stopping. Urging Lily on faster until she was just fifty yards behind Joss, she leaned forward in her stirrups and yelled at Joss to take hold of one rein and turn Topper, knowing that if he started to circle, he would have to slow down.

But Joss was frozen in the saddle, clinging on, her stricken face white. With one final burst of speed, Lily drew almost level with the big Welsh and Georgia placed both reins into one hand, indicating to Joss what she wanted her to do. With the little mare beside him, and starting to tire, Topper started to follow Lily's lead. To Georgia's relief, his gallop slowed to a canter and he started to turn a large circle, allowing Joss to gain control of his reins again. His canter then slowed to a trot and finally both ponies ground to a shuddering halt, Topper slick with sweat, blowing his nostrils out, his eyes wide, showing the whites. He was *definitely* too much of a handful for Joss!

CHAPTER SEVENTEEN

"Th–thanks, Georgia, oh thank you…" All the smugness had disappeared from Joss's voice now.

"That's OK," Georgia said, her voice short. She was mad at Joss for putting both ponies in danger. Lily could have easily tripped and fallen, travelling at that speed, but seeing how scared Joss was, she felt her resolve weaken. There was nothing more frightening than a bolting pony. Thanking

Melanie silently, who had earlier made all three Redgrove riders attach a lead rope to their saddle in case of an emergency, she unclipped the rope and, leaning forward, fastened the clip on to Topper's bridle.

"What are you doing?" Joss said nervously.

"Making sure he doesn't do that again," Georgia said grimly. "Come on, let's get you both home."

There was little point in trying to catch up with the rest of the Pony Club riders. Georgia knew that if they followed the edge of the woodland back towards Redgrove it would bring them out on the little back track leading down to Dan's farm. From there it was only a mile or so home to Seven Birches, but they needed to hurry. The snow had started to fall again, small flakes drifting downwards as Georgia and Lily led the weary Topper back home. As they reached the edge of the woods and the bridleway, the snow was falling faster, big heavy flakes settling on the ponies' manes and quickly turning the countryside white. The air was strangely quiet as the ponies trudged along, and so were both riders. Georgia couldn't think of anyone she wanted to talk to less than Joss, and so she concentrated on the task ahead, delivering both pony and rider safely home. When she had a decent mobile signal she rang Melanie, who suggested they wait at Dan's farm and she would pick them up from there.

Georgia looked guiltily at the missed calls from Sophie. With all the drama of Topper bolting, she had completely forgotten to let her friend know that she would make her separate way home.

Georgia had never been so grateful to turn into the small track that led down to Dan's farm. The snow was thick and she could barely see her hands holding the reins now. Joss had already called a groom from Seven Birches, who was on his way, ready to whisk Topper and Joss back to the warmth and safety of the plush stables. Georgia wasn't so lucky. Hearing her mobile ring, she peeled off a frozen glove and answered, her teeth chattering with cold.

"Georgia, I'm so sorry." Melanie sounded panicked. "The lorry won't start. It must be the freeze, and Simon can't get the trailer off the drive without slipping everywhere. I'm so sorry, we just can't get to you." She paused. "Please don't attempt to ride home in the snow."

"Don't worry." Georgia tried her best to assure Melanie. "I'm sure I can put Lily in the stable here, and Mr Coleman is probably about." But her heart sank as Melanie continued. She had already rung Dan's dad on his mobile, only to find out that he and Dan's older brother Ben were out clearing snow in the village with their tractor.

Dan was still helping clear up after the mock

hunt and was going to hitch a ride home a bit later. Georgia would have to wait alone until someone arrived back. Leaning forward and unclipping Topper, Georgia guided the two weary ponies into the yard and both riders breathed a huge sigh of relief.

The farm was very quiet. Apart from the odd low moo coming from the cows' winter barn, there was an odd silence. It took Georgia a moment or two to realise it was *too* silent. Normally, Hattie would have bustled up by now, or she would have heard Dan's sheep. Listening carefully, Georgia heard the faint whimper of Dan's collie. She frowned and looked around. Where was Hattie? The whimper grew louder, accompanied by a short, shrill bark. Hattie was trapped somewhere!

Jumping off Lily and quickly running the stirrups up, Georgia told Joss to stay where she was. Hattie had probably been accidentally locked in one of the buildings in Mr Coleman's haste. It wasn't the first time it had happened – Hattie loved seeking out mice in the sheds, and Dan always joked that her hearing was selective.

The snow was still falling but the earlier whiteout had subsided, with only a few small flakes drifting down. In the short time it had been snowing, it had been enough to thickly carpet the farmyard, and Georgia's riding boots were almost covered. The whimpering was louder now, and Georgia quickly realised it was coming from the little stable where Secret had been born. Smiling to herself, she imagined Hattie wandering in and having a sleep on the deep straw bed, until to her horror she saw that a metal bar had been placed across both doors, jamming them shut. As she heard Hattie whine and yip at the sound of Georgia approaching, she felt a shiver run down her spine as she realised Hattie had been deliberately trapped in the stable.

Wrenching the bar back, Georgia dragged the stable door open and freed an ecstatic, joyful Hattie, who weaved excitedly in and out of Lily's and her legs. The palomino gazed down at the collie with mild interest. Thinking quickly, Georgia quickly led Lily round the side of the stable, her heart sinking into her boots as her suspicions were confirmed. The gate to the sheep barn was wide open and, judging from the trampled snow in front of the entrance, leading off to the right, the sheep had only recently exited. Georgia had an image of Dan's devastated face in her mind, as she envisaged him finding out his beloved flock had gone. She swiftly led Lily back round to the main farmyard, where Joss was now standing by as the groom from Seven Birches rugged and loaded Topper.

"Joss…" Georgia's voice was breathless. "Please

stay and help me. I think Dan's sheep have been stolen."

Joss looked only mildly interested as she read a message on her mobile phone. "What can I do about it?" she said with a hint of annoyance. "Look, Georgia, I'm completely exhausted and I'm freezing out here. I really want to get home for a bath."

Georgia couldn't believe it! Joss obviously didn't care about Dan at all. She glared at the pretty actress, trying to think of how to respond.

"Sorry, Georgia," Joss continued, flicking back her hair as she climbed into the warmth of the cab. "I've got to go. I've got a party to get to."

And without another word, the horsebox pulled out of the driveway and purred into the lane, leaving Georgia and Lily alone in the yard, staring at the back of the disappearing vehicle.

CHAPTER EIGHTEEN

There was no time to feel sorry for herself. After trying Dan's mobile, which went straight to voicemail, Georgia remounted Lily and rode back round to the barn, thinking over her options. The snow was soft and powdery. The sheep couldn't have gone far; the prints in the snow were fresh.

"Come on, Lily."

The little palomino seemed to sense what

Georgia wanted and, snorting into the cold air, set off on the trail of the flock, guided by Georgia, who squinted into the fading afternoon light, trying to spot any movement. She had ridden the fields behind the farm enough to know the sheep were heading out towards the little back road that lay between the farm and the village of Redgrove. She remembered Dan's worries over his sheep being stolen, and shook her head. Surely that hadn't happened, or were his fears justified? Hearing a little bark beside her, she looked down and noticed Hattie lolloping next to Lily, grinning up at her, her tail wagging. Georgia felt a wave of gratitude towards the little dog. "Come on, girls," she said determinedly as she nudged Lily into a canter. "Let's get these sheep back."

As the trio rounded the corner and started to head towards the furthest point on the farm, where the fields met the boundary, Georgia caught her breath as she saw a silver livestock vehicle partially hidden in the lane. The gate leading on to the lane was wide open and, even worse, the sheep were heading straight towards it, flanked by a brown and white collie that was darting around, yapping with excitement. Georgia gave a small cry of horror as she noticed Dan's favourite ewe limping badly at the back of the group, her two tiny lambs trailing next to her. She looked terrified and bewildered, and Georgia felt her anger grow.

Quickly judging the distance between the gate and Lily, she flew into a gallop, aiming to cut across the path of the flock and stop them heading out into the lane. The snow was deep, but Lily ploughed through, sending up flurries of powder. They came to a sliding halt in front of the gate. Georgia had no idea how to instruct a sheepdog to carry out its work, but waving her whip at

165

the brown collie she shooed it backward. For a fleeting moment she was aware of two dark figures running in the lane, and caught a glimpse of a surly-looking man, the same man Georgia had given directions to. For an awful moment, Georgia felt alone and terrified. But the two men whistled for their dog and sprinted towards the livestock lorry, pulling hoods over their faces as they went. There wasn't time to think about them; Georgia's priority was to get the frightened sheep home.

Reaching down and deftly swinging the gate shut, she tried to catch her breath, the freezing air catching in her throat. The sheep, now scattered, blinked at her as if in recognition but, still spooked, ran as Georgia approached them. They couldn't get on to the road but Georgia knew she had to get the lambs back into the warmth of the barn. Then she cried out as she noticed the sick ewe, Dan's favourite. She had stumbled forward and was lying heavily on her side, her lambs bleating pitifully next to her. Jumping off Lily, Georgia ran and knelt beside the loyal sheep, who was uttering short gasps, her eyes half closed. There was nothing Georgia could do, and tears sprang into the corners of her eyes as she gently cradled the ewe's head, remembering how Dan loved her and how she followed him everywhere, trotting along, bleating happily. The sheep's breathing became calmer and she gazed up at Georgia with a soft expression. With one last shuddering breath, her body relaxed and her dark eyes became fixed and glassy.

Crying, Georgia placed her head gently down into the snow and put her arms around Hattie, who was sitting next to her in silent solitude. Lily, sensing the sheep had died, hung her head and blew gently out of her nostrils. Suddenly the frightened little cry of the lambs jolted Georgia to her senses. Giving the ewe a final pat, she stood up. She had to get the rest of the flock safely back, and she needed to act quickly.

"I'm sorry, girl," she whispered.

It was horrible leaving her out there, lying in the snow, but Georgia had no choice. She couldn't physically carry her. The lambs nosed the still-warm fleece of their mother. Gathering them both up, their little bodies cold and their long legs wriggling, Georgia tucked them inside her open tweed coat, trying to warm them. They were freezing, and needed warmth and milk, fast. Suddenly Georgia had a brainwave. She remembered reading in one of her pony books that native ponies such as Highlands and Fells were used to bring deer and sheep down off the moor, before they became riding ponies and show ponies. Perhaps Georgia's special Welsh pony could do the same job! Very gently, she laid the two lambs carefully over the front of Lily's saddle, and gingerly swung herself up, so she could hold the lambs steady with her hands and guide Lily back using her legs.

Despite the sadness of the situation, Georgia couldn't help the corners of her mouth lifting into a smile as Lily flicked her ears back, bemused by her extra passengers. One week a winning show pony at Olympia International Horse Show, the next a shepherd pony! The little palomino seemed completely unaffected by the lambs on the saddle. Now there was just the rest of the flock to take care of, but somehow, sensing Lily's calmness, they had gathered behind her. Hattie, automatically doing her job, and used to bringing in the sheep with Dan, followed at the back, her eyes bright as she gently guided the little flock into a group.

"Right," Georgia said out loud, wondering how surreal they must have looked. "Homeward!"

Meanwhile, back at the farm, Mr Coleman and

Ben were standing in the yard, a panicking Ben dialling the number of the local police station. Suddenly Mr Coleman placed a hand on his arm, urging him to look out towards the fields. Both rubbed their eyes, wondering if they might be imagining things. Coming towards them was a small figure in a tweed coat hunched over two tiny lambs, on the saddle of the most famous Welsh Section B in the country! Followed by thirty placid ewes and their missing collie.

"What the—" Mr Coleman, normally so bustling and cheerful, was completely lost for words, as Ben just gaped at the funny-looking group.

"Georgia?" he said, his voice full of a hundred questions.

"No time," Georgia said urgently. "I don't know anything about sheep, but I think these two need some help." She gestured to the weakening lambs lying quietly across the saddle.

Mr Coleman nodded. "Ben," he ordered his older son. "Get heat lamps and blankets, and make up some bottles."

Ben hurried off to the house as Mr Coleman gently lifted the weak lambs off the saddle and cradled them. "Where's the mother?" he said, looking at Georgia. "We need to get them back together."

Georgia shook her head sadly. "I'm sorry," she whispered, hanging her head, and Mr Coleman understood straightaway.

"I'll go and collect her," he said quietly. A farmer for his whole life, Mr Coleman could be tough at times but he adored his animals.

With the rest of the flock safely back in their barn and Lily in the old goat stable, Ben set up the heat lamp in the smaller stable next to her. Lily hung her head over the low stone partition and watched with interest as Ben set to work rubbing the babies down with a blanket, trying to warm them up. Mr Coleman had managed to find an old stable rug buried under a pile of junk in the outside garage. It was a bit musty but Georgia was just grateful that Lily would be warm after her ride to the rescue in the snow. The little mare had once again shown how brave and willing she was, even after a long day at the mock hunt. Placing her arms around Lily's neck, she silently willed the two orphan lambs to survive.

"Dad? Ben?" A quad bike roared into the farmyard and Dan leapt off and ran into the stable, taking in the sight of Lily and Georgia, as well as Ben crouching down beside the two lambs.

Ben placed a finger to his lips. "They're OK, Dan," he said as Mr Coleman joined them carrying two warm bottles of milk. "It's all thanks to this very brave girl," he said, winking at Georgia, who blushed.

"W–what?" Dan shook his head. "I don't understand."

"Sit down," Ben said, handing him one of the bottles. "Georgia will tell us everything, but we need to get these two fed."

CHAPTER NINETEEN

As Georgia recounted the tale, from finding the barn open and the sheep missing, to discovering poor Hattie locked in, Dan listened quietly, cradling the smaller of the lambs as it eagerly suckled the bottle of milk. Georgia told him straightaway about the ewe's death. She stumbled over the words, her voice catching as she described the friendly sheep falling to the ground. Dan lowered his head over the lamb lying in his arms. He didn't say anything but Georgia could hear him quietly sniffing.

Feeling desperately sorry for him, she placed her hand on Dan's shoulder, offering silent comfort. Finally, after a long moment, Dan lifted his head, wiped his eyes and gave a rueful smile. "Suppose I should be tougher, as a farmer," he said, his voice wavering. "But she was my favourite."

He was interrupted by his dad, who was resting his arms on the stable door. "Just gone to pick the old girl up," he said gently. "Poor thing. Died of shock, I expect." Then, turning to Georgia, he asked if she had caught sight of the men and the vehicle used. Georgia nodded, ready to give Mr Coleman an account of what she had seen, but Dan exploded.

"You didn't tell me this bit!" he said, sounding furious. "Georgia, you shouldn't have gone after them! You put yourself in so much danger!"

Georgia hung her head, scuffing her boots against the straw. "I know," she mumbled, "but I just wanted to get the sheep back for you." Looking up slowly, she saw that Dan's eyes were warm.

"It's OK," he said, gently this time. "I don't know if you are an idiot, or brave, but … thank you."

"It was mostly Lily." Georgia put her arms around the palomino's neck. "And Hattie."

Mr Coleman smiled weakly. "That wonder pony of yours," he said. "Saving the day again."

The lambs were now on their feet, looking stronger, their fleeces warm under the lamps and their tummies full of milk. Lily gazed down at them. She was a maternal mare, and Georgia wondered if she remembered giving birth to Secret in the very same stable. Satisfied that the sheep in the barn and the orphan lambs were doing well, Ben and Mr Coleman set off back to the house, leaving Dan and Georgia sitting next to each other in the straw.

"Georgia, I—" Dan began, just as Georgia opened her mouth to say Dan's name. They both laughed a little awkwardly.

"You first," Georgia smiled, but before Dan could answer, the mobile in his pocket rang, making him jump.

"Hello?" he said, pressing the phone to his ear. "Oh … hi, Joss…"

Georgia sank back on the straw as Dan continued his conversation. He was frowning. "Well, yes, they're OK, no thanks to you," he said before continuing. "No, I don't think so." There was a few moments' pause as he listened to the conversation, before ending with a terse, "Bye."

Dan looked straight at Georgia. "You didn't tell me Joss left you on your own to deal with the break-in?" he said, his voice stern.

"Well…" Georgia tried to think of an answer. "She said she had a party to go to … and she was pretty tired…" Her words trailed off as Dan gazed at her. "Anyway," she mumbled. "You should probably check she's OK, seeing as she's your girlfriend."

"Girlfriend?" There was a stunned silence, before Dan started laughing. "What on earth made you think that?" he said in amazement.

"Oh come on, Dan," Georgia said crossly. "It's fairly obvious!" And before she could stop herself she told him that she knew he had told Joss that he only saw Georgia like a sister. Plus there had been all the time that Dan and Joss had spent together at Olympia.

Dan shook his head, the laughter dying. "She said *that*? A sister?" He sounded angry, and Georgia nodded in reply, feeling embarrassed.

"Georgia!" Dan continued. "Joss told *me* that

you were hoping to get together with Will at the Pony Club party!"

There was a moment of awkward silence as they both tried to absorb what they had been led to believe.

Georgia spoke first. "But you did like her. You couldn't make that up." And it was Dan's turn to look embarrassed.

"I'll admit it was flattering at first, and I was so pleased about being in the film," he mumbled. "I just thought she was being friendly, but it started to get annoying. She's not like you, Georgia."

"So the time she was here," Georgia pressed, trying to ignore the last bit of Dan's answer. "At the farm?"

"I promise you," Dan said seriously. "She just turned up and invited herself into the shop. Ben was there. He thought she was rude. And you were acting so off and distant with me…"

Then Dan started laughing and, as mad as she was with Joss, she couldn't help but join in. She felt mortified but relieved all at the same time. Dan wasn't going out with Joss, and he did still like Georgia, maybe!

"But she's so pretty, and fun, and glamorous," Georgia said miserably, pulling apart a piece of straw.

Dan laughed, but his voice was warm as he spoke. "Maybe," he said sincerely. "But no one else I know would have done what you did tonight, Georgia," he said, drawing her in close.

Dragging her eyes upwards, Georgia could only see warmth on Dan's face.

"Going after my sheep like that, bringing the lambs back here... It was mad, but brave and amazing. *You're* brave and amazing." Reaching up, he patted Lily's muzzle as the little mare dozed with her head hanging over the partition. "You

and Lily!" he chuckled. "I don't know what I'd do without you."

Blushing, Georgia could only grin as Dan spoke. She couldn't think of the words to reply, but luckily any awkwardness was diverted by the smaller of the two lambs bleating as she tried to right herself on her long legs. "I think they're going to be OK," Dan said happily. "I can never thank you enough."

Dan and Georgia smiled at each other, an unspoken understanding passing between them. The lambs seemed calmer in the presence of Lily, who whickered softly as they tottered underneath her muzzle. She couldn't get in with them, but the partition between the stables was low enough for her to reach down and gently blow her sweet warm pony breath over the two tiny bodies.

At that moment there was the muffled sound of wheels crunching up the farm drive and, peeking

181

out, Georgia saw Melanie driving up in her 4×4. Emma and Will were sitting in the passenger seats, and as the vehicle came to a stop Sophie jumped out as well. Melanie was carrying an armful of rugs and, to Georgia's huge relief, a clean dry fleece jacket and a bobble hat.

"Georgia, I'm so sorry." Melanie opened the door of the stable. "There's no way we could get the lorry or the trailer off our yard."

Melanie explained that she had spoken to Mr Coleman, who had agreed that Lily could stay the night and Georgia could ride back in the daylight next morning, over the fields.

"A Christmas Day ride." Georgia smiled. "Perfect!"

News of the attempted theft had travelled fast. With Georgia's description, the police had stopped a suspicious-looking farm vehicle, heading slowly out of Redgrove on the roads Dan's dad and Ben had cleared, and arrested the two men. Georgia was pleased she had been able to help, but hoped the little collie was safe; it wasn't its fault that it was owned by criminals.

The Pony Club party at the manor house that was to follow the mock hunt had had to be cancelled due to the sudden snowfall but everyone was in a celebratory mood anyway, so Mr Coleman invited the group into the kitchen of the farm bungalow for a Christmas toast. Even Mrs Black was able to join them, chauffeured up to the farm by a cheerful Ben in the old farm Land Rover.

With her mum listening, Georgia decided to skim over some parts of the sheep rescue when describing her adventure; she didn't want to worry her. Looking back, she realised she had been a little reckless going after the sheep all by herself, but she had only been doing it for the sake of the animals, and for Dan. Whether or not they were just friends, or something more, Georgia would always go to his rescue if it was needed. Thinking of the sheep, she decided to go and check on the lambs and Lily as the impromptu Christmas party was in full swing.

Putting Sophie's bobble hat on over her ears, she stepped out into the freezing night. The snow was crunchy underfoot but the sky was illuminated by a thousand stars and there was no need for a torch as the moon lit up the yard. Switching on the light in the stable, she crouched down next to Lily, who was curled up on the straw bed. The lambs, tucked around one another, were asleep under the heat lamp and twitched slightly, their eyes closed. The stable was completely quiet.

Lily blinked as the light was turned on but stayed down even as Georgia sat beside her, placing her arms around her neck. There was something quite

184

magical about sitting in a stable with her beloved pony on Christmas Eve.

Giving a low rumbly whicker, Lily looked up as Dan quietly approached, letting himself in and sitting next to Georgia in the straw. They sat in contented silence for a while, as Lily closed her eyes and lay her head in Georgia's lap, the distant sounds of carols from the village church carrying over on the cold night air.

"What a month!" Dan smiled, breaking the silence. "Actually, scrap that – what a year!"

"I know," Georgia said, gently rearranging the little palomino's thick cream forelock. "I don't know how Lily will be able to top what she's achieved this year." She felt a little awkward all of a sudden.

Dan grinned. "We'll think of something," he laughed. "And whatever you do, you know I'll be here for you both." Leaning forward, Dan's lips gently grazed Georgia's as he gave her the sweetest, softest kiss. "Merry Christmas, Georgia Black."

Georgia felt a tingle run down her spine. Life couldn't get more perfect than this!

☆ ☆ ☆

A few days into the new year, and with the new school term looming, Georgia was in a reflective mood. What *did* the future hold for her and Lily? She thought back to her time at Josephine Smalley's yard, and remembered Josephine suggesting Lily should try her hand at dressage. Maybe it wasn't such a bad idea. It would be a new area for them to try. Georgia was still thinking this over as she rode back into Redgrove Farm on a loose rein after a brisk hack in the bright but chilly sunshine.

Tying Lily up outside her stable, quickly untacking her and putting her rug back on, her eyes were drawn to a pink sparkly parcel propped up against the stable door, and addressed to her. Curiously she tore the paper off, and to her surprise found the most beautiful framed headshot of Lily in her crystal bridle on the film set.

Turning it over, she found it had been signed by the entire cast, with an invitation to go to the premiere of the film. There was a scrawled note accompanying it from Joss.

"Dear Georgia," it read. *"Thank you so much for saving me when Topper bolted on Christmas Eve. He's at Hyde Park now and I'm having regular lessons to try and build the same relationship you and Lily have. I know it might take a while!*

Love, Joss

P.S. Say hi to Dan. He really likes you, you know."

A bemused smile crept on to Georgia's face. She had a strong feeling that Joss would have forgotten all about Dan in a few weeks. She was the kind of girl so used to having her own way – choosing

Lily, buying Topper, but she hadn't got Dan!

Laughing out loud, Georgia gave her little mare a hug. What a Christmas it had been – one she would never forget. Lily had proved her champion status, but, most importantly, now the film had finished and Olympia was over, things were back to normal. Georgia didn't know what the next year would hold for her and Lily, but she knew one thing – she could achieve anything with the palomino pony by her side and Lily's golden ears firmly pricked towards the future.

the PALOMINO PONY

ACKNOWLEDGEMENTS

Nosy Crow would like to thank Katy Marriott Payne for letting her lovely palomino pony star on the covers of this series.

If you liked this, you'll love

RED
MOON
RISING

PAULA HARRISON

Turn the page for a sneak peek!

Prologue

Ten years before

The child toddled down to the bottom of the garden and gazed at the grassy hill rising up on the other side of the gate. She looked through the bars and giggled. Black-winged figures flew over the top of the hill, outlined against the setting sun. They swooped and hovered as if they were dancing in the air. Spellbound, the little girl pulled at the latch and the gate creaked open.

A woman in a red dress ran down the path and scooped her up. "What are you doing out here, baby?"

The girl flapped her arms. "Fly, Mummy!"

The winged figures swooped even faster. A bright flash shot through the peaceful air and one of them crumpled before spiralling to the ground.

The woman ran inside, carrying the child with her, and locked the door. She set her daughter down gently and peered round the edge of the curtain, her face pale.

The little girl tugged at the hem of her mother's

skirt. Fine hair curled in wisps round her face. "Fly, Mummy?" she asked.

"Maybe one day, Laney." Her mother hugged her. "One day when we're far away from here."

CHAPTER 1

Laney opened her water bottle and took several big gulps. The water was warm and tasted sour like lemon juice. She lowered the bottle. For a second it looked as if the water was boiling, with big, fat bubbles rolling up to the surface. Then it was still.

Laney blinked. That was weird.

"Running round the track should be banned on the last day of term." Steph picked up her sports bag and stuffed her clothes into it. "Typical Miss Roderick, queen of PE torture."

Laney grinned and pushed back the fair hair that curled in wisps round her face. "Maybe they put that in her job description: *Must own a disgusting red tracksuit and enjoy making people suffer!*"

"They got exactly what they wanted then," said Steph.

The changing-room door banged as some of the other girls left.

Still thirsty, Laney decided to try another tiny swig of water to see how it tasted. As she tipped up the bottle, she caught a shadowy movement from the corner of her eye. The bottle was knocked out of her hand. Water splattered over her face and dripped down her clothes on to the changing-room floor.

"Oh, Laney!" said Jessie with mock sweetness. "Did I bump into you? I'm *so* sorry!"

Laney glared. "What did you do that for?" She

should have known it would be Jessie, and the gleam in the other girl's eyes showed exactly how sorry she was.

"It was just an accident." Jessie shook back her dark curls and flounced out of the changing room.

"Are you OK?" said Steph. "I don't know *what* is wrong with that girl."

"Don't worry about it. Jessie's been mean to me ever since nursery school. It's like part of her daily routine or something, and I didn't want that water anyway. It tasted really weird." Laney picked up the bottle. "I'm going to fill this up from the water fountain." She bent down to close her bag. At least her books had escaped getting wet.

As she straightened up she noticed Claudia watching her from across the changing room. As their eyes met, she gave Laney a half-smile and turned away to brush her hair.

Laney picked up her bag, staring curiously at Claudia, but the other girl didn't turn round again. Over the last few weeks she'd caught Claudia studying her a few times. She found it weird because Claudia was one of those cool types who'd never seemed to notice her before. She pushed through the changing-room door with Steph behind her. They walked down the corridor and through another set of doors to find Jessie and a bunch of her adoring fans hanging round the water fountain.

Laney was annoyed when her stomach lurched. She wasn't going to let Jessie stop her doing what she wanted.

"Better be quick. I think the bell's about to go." Steph hung back by the doors.

Laney's wet clothes stuck to her skin as she weaved her way through the group of girls and stopped in front of the fountain. She took the lid off the bottle and then dropped it. Cheeks flushing, she hurried to pick it up. Shaking the last drips out of the bottle, she pushed down the tap to turn on the fountain.

"How come you're thirsty, Laney?" said Jessie. "Is it hard work coming last round the track all the time? Don't worry, you can't help being a freak of nature."

Laney gritted her teeth as she watched the water trickle into the bottom of the bottle. She wasn't going to let Jessie have the last word. "If I'm a freak then so are you!" It wasn't a very good insult, but she couldn't think of anything better.

As she glared at Jessie, the bottle leaped in her hand and the water inside started to bubble.

"Watch it!" cried Jessie. The sneering look slipped from her face and her dark eyes widened. "What are you doing? Give me that! Get away from the fountain!" Her voice held a surprising note of panic. She tried to grab the water bottle but Laney held on to it tightly.

The bottle filled to the top and hot water splashed over their hands. The liquid inside was boiling and there was a strange, bulbous cloud of steam rising above it. The water looked beautiful, spilling out and swirling round the fountain plughole. It reminded Laney of something that she couldn't quite grasp. A memory, maybe. A forgotten moment in time.

Jessie backed away, her eyes narrowing. "What have you *done*?"

"Why's the water hot?" said Laney. "It shouldn't be hot." She reached forwards, dreamlike. As her fingers touched the fountain tap she felt a sudden jolt, like electricity, run up her arm.

A deep boom echoed along the corridor and time seemed to slow down as the tap exploded and the fountain split right off the wall. Water gushed from the exposed pipes in the wall and ceiling, flooding the passage in a matter of seconds.

Laney slipped, landing in the flood. Girls screamed, trying to shield themselves from the jets of spraying water. Jessie elbowed past them to be the first to the door.

Strangely calm, Laney watched them all struggling to get away. Classroom doors were flung open and people ran. The sharp voice of a teacher cut through all the shouting.

Laney got up, the water swirling round her knees. She must look so stupid – her clothes were properly soaked this time and she could feel her hair sticking to her forehead. She waded over to the door just as the metal water fountain was swept away down the corridor.

Blinding sunshine greeted her as she pushed her way through the exit, followed by a round of applause from all the kids gathered outside. Laney flushed again, feeling everyone staring at her.

"Right everybody, down to the field!" Miss Roderick rushed through the crowd in her red tracksuit. "Go to the place we use for fire drills."

"Why, Miss?" said Claudia. "It's not a fire, is it?"

"Just go where you're told, Claudia." Miss Roderick glared at her. "Hurry up, all of you! Away from the building." She hurried back and forth, rounding everyone up like a sheepdog.

Claudia stopped in front of Laney and fixed her with cat-like eyes. "What did you do in there?" she asked.

"What? Nothing!" Laney flushed. "The fountain broke."

Claudia stared unblinking for a few seconds. Then she turned in one smooth movement and joined the crowd heading for the field.

"The teachers won't blame you, will they?" said Steph nervously. "They might think it was an end-of-term joke."

Water suddenly broke through the doors and

gushed down the path, so the girls hurried away.

"I didn't do anything." Laney's voice shook. "How would I have got the fountain off the wall? There must've been a problem with the pipe or the water pressure or something."

"Well, you should know, as your dad does that sort of thing."

Laney thought for a moment. Her dad was a plumber, fixing pipes and mending leaks. She was sure he'd be able to explain why the pipes broke. What about the water in the bottle? It had looked just like it was boiling. And the tap on the fountain had exploded right at the moment she touched it.

But no one could boil water with their bare hands or make a tap explode just by touching it, could they?

A few hours later, with the water drained and the bottom corridor blocked off, the kids were allowed back in the building to fetch their things to go home. Laney kept her head down. If one more person thanked her for making them miss lessons, she thought she'd scream.

Miss Roderick caught up with her just outside the door. "Wait a minute, please, Laney. I've been told you were standing next to the fountain when it broke. Is there anything you can tell me about how it happened?" Her eyes searched Laney's face.

"It just came off the wall." Laney stared at the ground. She knew she should look at the teacher. She would only look guilty if she avoided her gaze. She had to remember she hadn't done anything wrong.

Well…not on purpose…